The First Day: Post Apocalyptic Thriller

Total Collapse: Day By Day, Volume 1

Adam Drake

Published by Adam Drake, 2020.

This is a work of fiction. Similarities to real people, places, or events are entirely coincidental.

THE FIRST DAY: POST APOCALYPTIC THRILLER

First edition. December 22, 2020.

Copyright © 2020 Adam Drake.

ISBN: 979-8201714468

Written by Adam Drake.

The First Day

And the end begins.

In one fell swoop, civilization is changed forever.

No one is unaffected, few are prepared.

Some become survivors, others - easy prey.

Only the strong, and crazy, will survive.

Through the blood and chaos, civilization will be permanently transformed.

And it all begins with one terrifying moment, when the lights go out and never come back on.

Total Collapse!

CHAPTER ONE

Nate

Pistol in hand, Nate Davenport eased through the bushes, then paused.

His eyes scanned over the backyard, an ocean of tall grass and weeds occasionally marred by an island of garbage. A child's swing set sat along one side by the fence, rusted from years of disuse.

Nate looked at the house. The windows of the two story derelict were boarded over, its back porch covered in leaves and dirt.

For several long moments, he waited. He'd learned from past mistakes not to rush headlong into a place he was unfamiliar. You can get into all sorts of trouble that way, especially when on a job.

Use your head, or I'll shoot it off!

He heard Unger's voice in the back of his mind. The boss loved to berate the men in his crew, even if they did a good job. A warped way of keeping people on their toes.

And it worked.

Nate checked his temper before it grew too hot. Focus, he thought. Get in, get it done, get out.

Satisfied no one was around, he slipped a nylon mask over his head and stepped out of the bushes at the back of the property line, then crossed the yard.

The high grass swished against his pant-legs as he navigated around piles of crap. The pistol was kept low at his hip.

Reaching the bottom step of the ruined porch, he paused. Not having the chance to scout the place ahead of time, he didn't know how creaky the old planks were.

Cautiously, he placed a foot on the first step.

A sudden noise made him freeze. He looked about in alarm.

A high pitched whirring sound echoed off the neighboring buildings. Apprehensive, he slipped his finger through the pistol's trigger guard.

The noise continued; whirring, grinding, clanking.

He recognized it. A garbage truck making its morning rounds down the street on the opposite side of the house.

The tension eased in his shoulders and he allowed himself to breathe again. Shouldn't have guzzled all that coffee earlier.

He climbed the stairs, with little noise and crossed the porch to the back door. It was ajar, the opening only revealing a wall of faded paint, beyond.

No one should be here. At least, according to Morse, the screw up. Unger's lackey was supposed to come by and check the place out first. Said it was all clear. Maybe he didn't even do a simple drive by.

That lazy bastard.

Nate's anger heated up like a bubbling volcano. He'd deal with Morse later.

Keeping to one side, gun at the ready, he pushed the door open.

Darkness and debris.

He tried to listen for movement, but all he could hear was the garbage truck; closer and louder.

After a few seconds of peering into the derelict's murk, he entered.

The place was empty of furniture. Dirt and garbage covered the cracked tile floor. A careful search of the bottom level came up with nothing. Why was the door ajar? Maybe a bum or junkie had spent the night and left.

Nate stopped at the stairs leading up to the second floor. No sign of movement or shadow play above.

The garbage truck was one house over, the sound almost deafening.

Keeping his back against the opposite wall, he climbed the stairs slowly. At the top was a hallway and a couple of bedroom doors, one wide open.

He checked the room with the open door and found it empty. A large broken window streamed in morning sunlight. Beyond was an apartment building.

With a quick glance behind him, he entered the room and sidled up to the edge of the window, and peeked out.

Directly across was another window, its curtains open showing a living room. A big screen tv on the far wall was playing a porno. Naked people jiggled about.

He could see chairs and a couch, but no sign of his target.

The sound of the garbage truck seemed to drown out the world. Damn, those things are loud.

The back of his neck prickled.

He spun around, pistol in both hands, its silencer barrel like a sword.

No one was there.

Nate took a second for his heartbeat to slow. He knew to never ignore that sensation. It had saved his life many times before and now he couldn't finish the job without being certain.

He reentered the hallway. Only the closed bedroom door on the opposite side confronted him.

Okay, then.

As he padded down the hall, a vibration at his hip brought him up short. Cursing inwardly, he fished out his phone while keeping the pistol pointed at the door.

He peered at the little phone's display.

Done yet?

It was Unger on a burner, checking in.

His eye twitched. What kind of moron sends text messages during a hit he ordered?

Nate knew he worked for an idiot. If not for Unger's incestuous family connections, the guy would have been encased in concrete or hanging from a tree by his intestines, long ago.

Ignoring his boss, he pocketed the phone and approached the door.

The garbage truck's angry presence outside reverberated through the old house.

Gingerly, he turned the door's knob then pushed it open.

Another bedroom. Empty, except for two problems.

A man and woman were laying on a foam mattress on the floor, both naked. Clothes scattered about, a pair of backpacks leaned against a wall.

The woman, early twenties, was out cold, snoozing. A colorful tattoo of a butterfly perched above the nipple of one breast.

A syringe stuck out of the arm of the man, who looked up at Nate and offered a groggy smile. "Hey, man...", he said. He blinked slowly, flying high.

Vagrants. Homeless. Bums. Whatever, Nate thought.

Outside the truck rumbled past, shaking the room's cracked window. No garbage worth picking up here.

Nate pointed the pistol at the man. "You shouldn't be here," he said.

The young man's drugged out state kept him from even registering the presence of the gun. "What?" he slurred. "I can't hear-."

Nate shot him in the forehead, the silencer coughing loudly, its noise suppressed further by the passing truck.

He shot the woman, too.

As he went back into the hall, he closed the door.

They'd been here all night. If Morse had done his job, Nate would have been informed. A new plan would have been made.

He and Morse were going to have a conversation later.

In the other bedroom, back at the window, he looked across.

A man was sitting on the couch, his back to the window. The porno still played out its fleshy antics, but with different actors this time.

Nate glared at the back of the man's bald head.

Perry Levine.

This twit got himself in debt with Unger. Something people with brains didn't do. After repeated attempts to collect, Unger, as usual, lost all patience and sent Nate to 'punch his card.'

Nate shook his head. Nobody has said 'punch his card' since the nineteen twenties. Except Unger, who liked watching old gangster flicks and emulated their characters.

I need a new job, Nate thought and aimed at Perry's head. It was like one of those shooting targets at the fair. Only this one would bleed.

The garbage truck had stopped outside the apartment building, and its keening grew louder as it loaded up.

Perfect, Nate thought. At least he had this going for him.

He slowed his breathing. In through the nose, out through the mouth. His hands steadied. The end of the silencer was pinned to Perry's skull.

He squeezed the trigger.

The garbage truck suddenly turned off.

Nate stopped pulling at the trigger. Shit.

The porno on the television winked out, the screen going black.

Perry reacted by moving about, probably looking for the remote, making for a messy target.

Double shit. Nate blinked in confusion at the loss of his covering noise and the sweet moment of splattering Perry's melon all over his living room.

Somewhere in the distance he heard a crash, the crunching of fiberglass and metal. Then another. Car accident?

Perry got up and walked over to the television. He wasn't wearing any pants, no doubt to better enjoy the porno.

Cursing again, Nate ducked out of view, back against the wall. What the hell was this?

Another crash, this one closer but the noise going on for several long seconds. Crunch-crunch-crunch. A car rolling over and over.

Far away, a woman screamed.

Okay, this was messed up. He needed to go. Now.

But he couldn't leave. You don't kill two people and not go through with the real job.

He looked out the window, again.

Half-naked, Perry now stood facing toward the window, but he was frowning down at a smart phone in his hand.

Good enough, Nate thought. He aimed, this time at the center body mass.

Perry shook his head as if totally confused by the phone. Then he must have sensed something and looked up.

His eyes locked with Nate's, then to the pistol in his hands. His eyes widened.

Another crash, just on the street outside like someone drove into the garbage truck.

Nate fired. Two loud coughs and Perry's window cracked with the double slugs.

Perry fell backward with a muffled cry and vanished from view.

Without wasting another second, Nate moved from the window, scooped up the two spent casings and left the bedroom. At the bottom of the stairs, he paused. There was shouting from close by, but none from the apartment building. Not yet.

At the back door, he looked outside. Satisfied it was all clear, he slipped his pistol into the deep pocket of his long coat, and stepped onto the porch.

Despite the hammering of his heart, he had the presence of mind to close the door quietly behind him. Less of an invitation for other drug-addled backpackers. He calmly crossed the backyard. His growing anxiety made it feel like the tall grass was trying to slow him down, force him back to the scene of his crimes.

He gently pushed through the bushes at the back of the property line and out into the back alley. More a gravel road than a real alley, it went north and south.

Slipping off his nylon mask, he turned south and sauntered along, gravel crunching underfoot. To a casual observer he would appear to be an average joe out for a walk, and not a paid hitman with three fresh bodies in his wake.

As he emerged from the gravel lane, and onto a paved cross street, movement in the sky made him stop in his tracks.

To the south, the landscape dipped downward, giving him a relatively clear view of the downtown core in the distance, with its clusters of skyscrapers and office buildings.

A large passenger plane was gliding earthward, heading toward downtown at a fatal angle.

"Huh," Nate said. "Ain't that a sight." Then he turned away and walked to his car.

CHAPTER TWO

Wyatt

"What kind of money do you think we can get for a dead body?"

Wyatt, who was busy arranging bags of cans in his cart, paused and looked up at his friend, Ethan. "What the hell kind of question is that?"

Ethan was perched on the edge of a dumpster, legs swung over inside, ready to drop in and start hunting for recyclables. "It's a legitimate question considering I'm looking right at one."

"No, you're not," Wyatt said and looked both ways down the alley. The garbage truck was late which suited him fine. He and Ethan weren't done with their rounds, yet. "There is no dead body. You just don't want to work. It is your turn. We switch at the next alley over."

Ethan stared into the dumpster and frowned. With his long white beard the expression made him look like a depressed Santa Claus. "I'm not looking to skip my turn. I'm just curious if maybe we could profit from this fella's misfortune."

Annoyed, Wyatt dropped a shopping bag of cans into the cart with a loud clatter, and moved to the dumpster to peer over its edge.

Sure enough, the body of a man was nestled in amongst full garbage bags as if he were sleeping. But the wide vacant eyes and ashen skin made this sleep eternal.

"Well, I'll be damned," Wyatt whispered, shocked.

"Told you," Ethan said. "What should we do with him?"

Wyatt tore his gaze away from the body to look at Ethan. "Do with him? Why, nothing at all. That's what we do with him. What makes you think we should do anything other than get the hell out of here?"

"Well, he's in our dumpster, so technically he's ours."

"This is not our dumpster. It's the apartment building's. Just because we dive into it every morning doesn't make the thing ours." Wyatt pointed a finger at the dead man. "And that makes this guy the apartment manager's problem."

Ethan shook his head. "Wyatt, buddy. You're such a negative-Nancy. But you're right, this is not our problem."

"Damn right it's not!"

"It's our opportunity!" Ethan said and dropped inside the dumpster.

"What the hell are you doing?" Wyatt said, glancing toward the apartment building. He hoped no one came out right then, or they'd be screwed. "Get out of there!"

Ethan shifted some bags around to get a better look. He seemed absolutely fascinated with this find.

The dead man appeared to be quite young, maybe in his early twenties. He wore a dark blue jacket over a black dress shirt and black jeans. There was a tattoo on the back of one curled hand. Wyatt recognized its symbol.

"He's a Feral Kid," Wyatt said with disgust. Maybe it was good this guy was dead. The Feral Kids were a notorious homeless gang that roamed the city, terrorizing and extorting the other homeless. Wyatt had many encounters with them over the years, none of which were pleasant.

"Yeah, you're right," Ethan said, leaning closer.

"Can you tell how he died?" Wyatt asked, curious despite himself.

"Being a Feral Kid is how he died, I'd guess. Not the most work safe occupation you can choose." Ethan delicately lifted open the man's jacket. "I don't see any blood, but there's too much crap in here to tell."

"I don't think you should be touching him, Ethan."

"Why not? He won't mind." Ethan reached into the man's shirt pockets and felt around.

"God damnit! What are you doing? You're gonna get your DNA all over him. What about forensics?"

Ethan shifted to jam his fingers into the man's jean pockets. "DNA. Forensics. What's that all mean to people like us? No one cares. This guy will be scooped up by the truck and ferried off to the dump. He'll end up under tons of shit and will rot away to nothing with the rest of the garbage."

Wyatt stepped away from the dumpster to check the alleyway, again. Other than a dozen dumpsters full of their morning trash there was no one around. He tried listening for the garbage truck but couldn't make out its distinctive sound.

"This isn't good, Ethan. I don't like it. Come on, get out of there. We'll skip this row and go to the next alley over."

Ethan didn't find anything and scratched at his chin, disappointed. "They picked him clean, whoever did this. There isn't even lint in his pockets." He spotted the man's shoes. "Oh, hey! Check these kicks out!"

Wyatt looked on in horror as his friend wrestled a pair of faded runners off the dead man's feet. Not a sight he expected to see when he woke up in his tent that morning to start his rounds. He expected more of the same. Cans, bottles, and the reek of garbage filled dumpsters.

It had been his routine for the last eight years. Day in and day out. Not once did he encounter a dead body. Dead animals, sure. Rats, and cats, and even a dog or two. But not a person. Feral Kid or not, this guy had been a human being. Watching Ethan casually manhandle the body suddenly made him queasy.

Somewhere from down deep, a memory fought to surface. "Oh, I think I'm gonna be sick," Wyatt said and stumbled over to throw up behind the dumpster. Cold coffee and stale bagels.

Ethan dropped to the ground, the dead man's runners on his feet. "Now your DNA is everywhere. We're both going to hang."

Wyatt wiped his mouth with the back of his sleeve and glared at his friend. "Satisfied?"

"With the runners? Damn right. They fit perfectly!"

Wyatt opened his mouth to berate Ethan when the sound of a distant car crash tore his attention away.

They both turned in the direction of the noise. It was immediately followed by another crash, metal smashing against metal.

"Damn," Ethan said pacing around in his runners, trying to break them in. "Someone was in too much of a hurry to get somewhere."

Another crash, this time from the other end of the alley. From that direction a woman screamed.

"We're at the epicenter!" Ethan said.

"What? This isn't an earthquake, just shitty drivers hopped up on caffeine." Wyatt scoffed and grabbed the dumpster's heavy lid.

"What are you doing now?"

"Laying him to rest," Wyatt said and eased the lid closed. "Have any last words?"

"Yeah, I'd like to thank the guy for wearing size twelves."

"Let's get out of here," Wyatt said grabbing the cart full of cans. "The less time here the better."

Ethan grabbed the other cart which they used to carry glass items. Only a half dozen beer bottles rattled at its bottom.

They pushed their carts down the middle of the alley trying to not look suspicious.

"Why'd they kill him?" Ethan asked. He kept grinning down at his new shoes having tossed his old pair in the cart.

"I haven't the foggiest," Wyatt said. He kept glancing at each of the dumpsters they passed. All probably filled with cans and bottles. The truck would be by soon and would haul them off to the dump. What a waste of money.

Ethan didn't appear to mind all the missed out treasure they were passing. At least he got something out of this run. "Bet you it was over drugs. Drugs and guns. It's always over drugs and guns."

They walked on for several minutes, cans and bottles rattling.

"Money," Wyatt finally said. "Probably money."

"Yeah, but drugs and guns get you the money."

"Or money gets you the drugs and guns."

They chuckled.

Wyatt felt strange laughing. They'd found a dead body, robbed it, and left it to cook in a dumpster under the morning sun. He shouldn't be laughing.

As they came to the end of the alley, they both stopped. The cross street in front of them was littered with cars.

Vehicles had stopped everywhere in the middle of the street and along its sides. Some even on the sidewalks.

A slick looking car had jumped the meridian and crashed into a concrete divider. A Chinese man stood next to its open driver-side door helping a woman inside who was wedged behind an air bag. She looked dazed.

"Well, fuck a duck," Wyatt said, agog.

Ethan made a tsk-tsk sound. "Everybody in too big of a damn hurry." He turned his cart onto the sidewalk and pushed on. Wyatt followed still a little stunned at the odd carnage around him.

"What do you think happened?" Wyatt said.

"Don't know, don't care," Ethan said as he steered around a sedan which had driven over the sidewalk and buried itself in a line of thick hedges. "If it becomes our concern, I'll let you know."

Ethan didn't like people and did his utmost to avoid them. And by people, that meant those with more money than him.

Which meant everybody.

Wyatt couldn't blame him. The crap they both had to put up with as dumpster divers could make you crazy. It continually disappointed him how folks sometimes treated those in need. To most, the homeless were less than the dog shit they scraped off the bottom of their shoe.

Still, Wyatt felt a little bad for that woman in the car. He even felt bad for the dead Feral Kid they'd left in the dumpster. Somewhere, this young man's parents were wondering where he was. Perhaps it was best they didn't know.

"Oh, crap," Ethan said, stopping.

"What? What is it?"

"Frikken Baldy," Ethan said, nodding further ahead.

Approaching them down the sidewalk, pushing a cart full of cans, was another homeless man. Unlike Wyatt and Ethan, he didn't have a beard or any hair for that matter as he was completely bald. Other than being known for his naked scalp he was also infamous for being completely insane.

Baldy spotted them and waved, a wide grin on his dirty face.

"Crap, here he comes," Ethan said.

"He's not all bad," Wyatt said. He didn't mind Baldy as long as he kept his crazy talk down to a low simmer.

"Bad enough," Ethan whispered as Baldy rattled up to them. "He Baldy! Top of the morning to you!"

"T-top of the m-morning to you, t-too!" Baldy said. His grin grew so comically wide it stretched from ear to ear.

"Morning, Baldy," Wyatt said, nodding. He gave Baldy's cart a once over. It was jammed full of cans, even more than what Ethan and he had dredged up that morning. Crazy or not, Baldy always knew where the fattest dumpsters could be found.

"D-did you see the p-plane?" Baldy exclaimed, excited. He blinked frantically as if he couldn't believe the words he was saying.

"Huh?" said Ethan.

"Th-the p-plane that crashed!" Baldy said and pointed to the southeast.

All of them looked in that direction. High buildings and tall trees blocked their view of any crash.

"I don't see nuthin," Ethan drawled. He didn't bother hiding his impatience.

Wyatt shrugged. "How do you know a plane crashed?"

"S-saw it coming d-down," Baldy said. "Into the d-downtown area."

"Uh-huh," Ethan said, turning to Wyatt. "Let's get going. We still need to cash these in and go eat."

Baldy looked confused, but didn't protest as both men steered their carts past him. "M-maybe we should h-help," he called after them.

"Oh, for Christ's sake," Ethan said.

Wyatt said, "Cops will take care of it, Baldy, don't you worry. Oh, and don't bother fishing the next alley up. We already cleaned it out."

Baldy nodded enthusiastically, but didn't move. He watched them as they walked on.

"Why did you say that to him?" Ethan asked, scowling.

"I don't want him finding that body. Who knows how he'd react."

Ethan scoffed. "Hell. How do we know he wasn't the one who put him there?"

"Baldy? He wouldn't hurt a fly." Mentally, Baldy was like a little kid and Wyatt did his best to look out for him. He just couldn't be around him for too long. That stutter drove him up the wall.

Ethan shook his head. "You can't read people at all, then."

"Why do you say that?"

"Cause Baldy has the crazy eyes. He's killed before. You can tell."

Wyatt shook his head, but didn't want to argue with Ethan, the eternal cynic.

They pulled off the street and into the next alleyway, a part of their route. Fourteen dumpsters eagerly awaited to be pried open like virgins on their honeymoon.

"Hopefully there won't be any bodies in these," Ethan said with a wry grin.

"Bodies?" someone said from behind them.

They turned.

Three scary looking young guys emerged from behind a fence where they'd been drinking beer.

"What bodies are you talking about?" said the taller of the three.

Icy fear washed over Wyatt. He didn't need to see the symbols tattooed on their hands to know who these guys were. He recognized each of them.

Feral Kids.

CHAPTER THREE

Nate

Approaching a getaway car always made Nate more nervous than it should. If someone wanted to ambush him, this was the perfect spot to do so.

Unger giving him this job, and assigning the idiot Morse to do the ground work, gave Nate pause. Maybe Nate was the job, or meant to be rolled up with it.

He tried to shrug away his doubts. Hitman jitters.

More shouts, this time from all around him.

"My God! That plane!" a man yelled from his yard, pointing. He'd been trying to start his lawnmower, but it wouldn't cooperate.

Nate kept his head low, concentrating on the sidewalk. Can't have people identifying him a block from a triple homicide. He needed to keep a low profile until he got some distance. Tough to do when you're over six feet and built like a Russian shot putter, but he did his best.

Another block, and more people began to emerge from their houses and apartment buildings, adding to his nerves. Some looked in the direction of the huge plume of smoke which now spiraled upwards from downtown. Others gaped like fish in confusion.

You'd think everyone would be tired of planes crashing into buildings after New York, he mused. Yet, this was also a good thing for him. Now their focus, and memory, would be of the plane crash, not of the large hitman who tromped past their home.

He approached a T-intersection where a bunch of cars and trucks had suddenly decided to park in the middle of the street. But as he got closer, he noticed that nearly all of them were mashed up against one another, side panels and bumpers dented, headlights shattered.

Drivers and passengers yelled at each other. Small crowds formed at the street corners, ogling the mayhem.

Nate kept walking. Why hadn't he parked closer? He shook his head. No, that would have been stupid. The rule was golden. For a stealth job, always keep your escape vehicle at least two blocks distance.

As he marched past the fender-bender carnage, a thought struck him. Why weren't there any sirens? No emergency vehicles racing to the scene. In fact, he didn't recall hearing any earlier after all those crashes.

He glanced southward. The thick pillar of smoke had grown larger stretching up into the sky. Maybe everyone was down there?

A half-block later, he had to walk around a mini-van that had jumped the curb and was perched over the sidewalk. A man sat in the driver's seat, his door open. He was cursing as he tried turning the key in the ignition over and over, but the engine appeared dead.

Nate noticed several vehicles similarly parked – up on sidewalks, in the middle of lawns, facing the wrong way in the oncoming lane. People cursed or looked confused, or both.

A skinny guy with a beard stood outside another mini-van which sat on the low concrete meridian in the middle of the street. Two brats cried inside. He frowned at his smartphone, pressing at it angrily.

Mr. Beard spotted Nate walking by. "Hey! Can I use your phone?"

No, but I got two bullets that'll solve that crying problem of yours, Nate wanted to say. Instead, he shrugged, non-committal, and kept going. Mr. Beard turned to yell at his brats.

Normally, he would have been annoyed, even alarmed Mr. Beard had made eye-contact with him, noticed him. But with all the strange chaos he doubted he was the most interesting thing people would remember that day.

Consider this a gift.

He imagined a prosecutor questioning Mr. Beard and pointing in Nate's direction. "Do you remember seeing this man on the morning of the fourteenth?"

Mr. Beard gave it some thought. "The fourteenth? The day that plane fell out of the sky? Wasn't that just terrible? And I couldn't get my phone to work!"

Nate chuckled at his own humor.

He spotted his car parked up ahead in the shade of some trees. Children played in a park nearby, a man threw a frisbee for a dog to chase.

No one else was around. Not anyone that might pop him one, anyway.

As he walked up to the driver's side, he glanced around one more time. Then he quickly unlocked the door and got in. After closing the door, he placed both hands on the steering wheel and took a deep breath.

Why was he so nervous? This certainly wasn't his first rodeo, he understood nearly every job made him a little apprehensive. But this one felt different. Was it Morse's sloppy scouting job, or the fact he got himself stuck working for Unger the idiot?

No. Something else.

He peered through the windshield. On the opposite side of the street a couple were standing on their lawn alternating their gaze from the black pillar of smoke to the phones in their hands.

Something was wrong. An amorphous thing he could not explain. And not just with the cars...

Curious, he stuck the key into the ignition and turned it.

Nothing.

He tried again. Same result.

"Ah, come on!" he said. After several more attempts it dawned on him that the seatbelt warning light hadn't blinked on. In fact, nothing on the dash lit up, as if the battery was dead.

Great, he thought. Now what? He was a couple of blocks from three people murdered by his own hand, with no way of making a quick escape.

He started to get angry and turning the key over and over again didn't help.

Giving up, he fished the phone out of his pocket. It was a disposable dumbphone, not a smartphone like all the idiots used. Can't get a GPS location on a dumbphone.

He thumbed a button, but the screen didn't turn on. He tried again. Nothing. He tried different buttons. The phone was dead. Yet, it had worked earlier.

Now he got really angry. Whatever affected everyone else had killed his car and made his dumbphone even dumber.

At least he didn't have to put up with Unger texting him with moronic questions.

Yes, the job is done, you twit. And no thanks to your flunky, Morse!

He pictured Morse's fat face as he bashed it in with his fist, over and over. Breaking the nose, knocking out teeth, causing his eyes to swell over and bruise. "There were people in the house!" he wanted to scream at him.

The thought made him feel a little better, soothing him.

With a sigh, he looked around. Okay, now what?

The couple across the street went back inside their house. The children kept playing, oblivious to the craziness of the day.

Feeling warm, he opened the door wide and propped his booted feet up on the concrete curb. He tried his dumbphone again to no avail.

Maybe he could steal a different car? This one wasn't even his, so why not grab another? But what if its battery was dead, too? How many cars would he go through until he found one that worked?

Could this get any worse?

The back of his neck prickled, and he scratched at it.

A shadow passed over him.

"Everything okay?" a female voice said.

Nate looked up, squinting.

Blue uniform, badge, and a holstered pistol.

Ah, crap, Nate thought.
A cop.

CHAPTER FOUR

Wyatt

"Did I stutter or something?" the Feral Kid asked. "When I ask a question, you answer."

Wyatt and Ethan gaped at the three thugs. Their sudden appearance in the alley caught the older men off guard. They'd never run into the Feral Kids on their rounds before. Usually, this particular kind of scum avoided residential back alleys.

Ethan froze up, his mouth working, but without any words spilling out.

Recovering from his surprise, Wyatt tried to look unimpressed. He knew the Kid who spoke. Went by the name Casket, of all things. He wasn't the big boss of the Feral Kids, more like a Captain. But assigning ranks to these kind of wild animals was giving them too much credit.

"Your name is Casket, right?" Wyatt asked.

Casket looked at Wyatt and sneered. "Yeah, that's my name, old man. What's yours? Dopey?"

His two friends chuckled. One had a scar across his chin and the other was missing all his upper teeth.

Casket grinned. "I mean, really, look at you two. You're like oversized dwarves or something with those beards, pushing your carts to go do some mining."

More chuckling from his friends. Wyatt noticed a large knife handle sticking out of Casket's waistband. Probably a Bowie-Knife judging from its size.

Wyatt very much wanted to get up in this punk's face. Take him down a peg or two. But he didn't think Ethan was up to the task of a fight. So he kept any insults to himself.

"Look," Ethan said, holding up his hands. "We don't want any trouble. We're just doing our rounds. We'll get out of your way."

Ethan started to push his cart, but Scarface blocked him.

Casket said, "What was this shit you were talking about? Bodies?"

Maybe these guys did it, Wyatt thought. Made sense. Here they were, a block away from where one of their own was stuffed in a dumpster. Or maybe they were out looking for him?

Either way, it spelled bad news for him and Ethan. These guys were looking for a fight, now that they had prey in their sights.

"We were talking about the plane crash," Wyatt said. He hitched a thumb southward. "The one that hit downtown. Lots of bodies. Understand, now?"

Casket blinked at Wyatt's explanation and shook his head. "What plane crash? There's no crash. You're just babbling shit so we don't stomp your ass."

Okay, Wyatt thought. So this is on. The icy fear faded away, replaced by anger. These guys expected an easy target. Well, with him, at least, they were in for a surprise. He tensed up.

Ethan's mouth sputtered to life. "Hey, we were just talking shit, you know. Heard about a crash. Maybe there is, maybe there ain't. Bodies, no bodies. We don't give a shit, we just want to go on our way."

Casket glared at Ethan and pursed his lips, acting like he was considering what Ethan said. "You know what, Sneezy, you're right. But if you want to pass, you got to pay a toll."

"Yeah?" Ethan said, skeptical, but relieved. "No problem. We got, uh, bottles and cans. Take what you want."

Casket nodded. "An interesting offer. But I'm not interested in your crappy shit, or your carts." He took a step closer to Ethan. "How much money you got?"

Oh, damn, Wyatt thought. Here we go.

"Money?" Ethan said glancing at Wyatt.

"Yeah," Casket said, glaring. "Cold hard cash."

Wyatt's temper grew red hot. "We work hard for what little we make. Besides, if you're going to extort us for pennies, do it after we've cashed in at the recycler, genius."

Casket's eyes widened and flexed his hands into fists.

"Not a problem," Ethan said, desperate to diffuse the situation. "Lemme just see what I got-." He didn't get to finish.

Casket's arm shot out and struck Ethan in the face.

Toothless was closest to Wyatt and made a move toward him, but Wyatt was already in motion.

From his pocket, Wyatt produced a pair of brass knuckles, having slipped them on while he was talking. He connected with Toothless' forehead as the young man tried to dodge away.

With an audible *thunk,* the Feral Kid dropped to the ground, out cold.

Ethan, for his part, was doing a valiant job of stopping Casket's fist with his face. Casket was raining blows on him over and over, driving Ethan backwards.

Scarface charged at Wyatt and tried to tackle him. Wyatt pushed a cart in his way and Scarface rammed into it, losing his balance.

As the Feral Kid tried to avoid falling, Wyatt cracked him in the nose with the brass knuckles. Cartilage crunched and Scarface's head snapped back. He dropped to the ground, squealing in pain and holding his face.

Wyatt turned to Casket.

Casket had Ethan up against a fence, but turned to face Wyatt, once he realized his two friends were down.

As Wyatt closed in on Casket, the Feral Kid whipped out the knife from his waistband. So it was a Bowie-knife.

Casket held it out daring Wyatt to get closer. "God damned Ninja-Hobo, huh?" he said, sneering.

Scarface and Toothless had recovered enough to stand, and they hobbled over to hover behind their leader. Neither looked as if they wanted to keep fighting.

Casket glanced at them and then to the determined look on Wyatt's face. He came to a wise conclusion.

"This isn't over, shitheads," Casket said, then slashed at Ethan's side. The razor-sharp blade easily cut through Ethan's shirt and made a deep gash. Blood gushed from the wound.

Ethan shrieked and peeled away from Casket to fall to the ground.

Wyatt saw red and took a step closer to Casket, but the knife kept him at bay.

"We'll finish this later, Dopey." Casket said, then the three of them turned and fled down the alley, vanishing around a corner.

Wyatt knelt beside Ethan. "Are you all right?"

Ethan's face was cinched up in pain. "No, I'm not all right! That bastard cut me!"

Wyatt looked at the wound. "He got you good, it looks deep."

"Feels pretty deep to me!" Ethan howled.

"Just a sec," Wyatt said, and went to his cart. He fished around for a few moments then came up with a small first-aid kit.

He returned to Ethan and opened the kit. Inside was a roll of gauze and some cue-tips.

Ethan managed a laugh. "Great. You can clean my ears as I bleed out."

"You are not going to bleed out," Wyatt said. He rolled up the gauze and gently pressed it against the wound. "Hold this here a second."

Ethan sputtered some curses as he held the gauze to his side.

Wyatt grabbed a long thin scarf from his cart. "Sit up, will ya?"

"Sheesh," Ethan said, leaning forward. "You're gonna have me moving cinder blocks, next."

Wyatt wrapped the scarf around Ethan's stomach. "Okay, exhale."

Ethan blew out an exaggerated breath then grimaced in agony as Wyatt tied the scarf over the gauze, holding it in place.

"Oh, sweet Jesus that hurts," Ethan said, sweating profusely. "Where did you learn to do this? Were you a combat medic in a former life?"

"Everything I know I learned from t.v.," Wyatt said, avoiding the other man's gaze. Everyone had secrets. He leaned back and looked Ethan over. "That should do for now."

Ethan wiped at his face, smearing blood over it. "Okay, now what, Ninja-Hobo?"

"I'll go get you some help," Wyatt said. "Find a phone and call for an ambulance." He turned to go.

"No, don't leave me here!" Ethan said, wincing in pain. "What if those idiots come back?"

Wyatt considered this for a moment. He'd hurt two of them pretty bad and were probably looking to get some medical help themselves. But Casket was unscathed. He might have only left to get reinforcements, then would come back looking for revenge. Which meant Wyatt couldn't leave Ethan here. Not with the slight chance of Casket returning.

"Okay," Wyatt said. "Let's get you up."

"Where we going?"

"Back down to the street," Wyatt said, putting one of Ethan's arms over his shoulder. "We'll find someone with a cellphone."

"No, no, wait!" Ethan said.

"What?"

"We're not leaving our carts here."

"Can't take them with us. God only gave me two hands."

Ethan gave the carts a forlorn look. "Okay, but at least hide them and lock them up. You still got that bike lock?"

"Yup," Wyatt said, easing Ethan against the fence.

He quickly moved the carts behind some nearby bushes and locked them together with the lock. Then he grabbed a small backpack which held his water bottle.

"Don't forget my bag!" Ethan said through gritted teeth.

"I wouldn't dare forget your man-purse," Wyatt said, snatching a small brown purse hidden in Ethan's cart and shoved it into the backpack. Whatever the purse contained was of grave importance to him.

"Happy now, you old goat?" Wyatt said, hoisting Ethan into a standing position, again.

"Never been happier, buddy," Ethan said as they hobbled down the alley. "Least I got myself some new shoes out of this deal."

"They are nice shoes," Wyatt said. His grin hid his concern. The wound was deep and Ethan was losing a lot of blood.

He needed to get his friend to a doctor, and quick.

CHAPTER FIVE

Nate

"What?" Nate asked, trying to get a better view of the cop who stood before him. The morning sun crested the rooftops of the houses behind her, blinding him.

"I wanted to know if everything was okay, Nate," the woman said.

Nate blinked at his name. She knew him? He felt a claw of ice grip his heart.

"Do I know you?" he asked, a little befuddled. He kept his expression neutral, calm. But inside he roiled with alarm. The situation had gotten much worse. Here he sat in a stolen vehicle, armed with an illegal weapon that could be linked to a trio of nearby bodies, speaking to a police officer who knew him by name.

Crap.

The cop stepped closer, blocking the sun and revealing her face. High cheek bones, a dusting of freckles, piercing green eyes.

The claw of ice tightened even more.

"Vicky!" Nat said, cavalier. "Long time, no see." He was still reeling inwardly at this rapid turn of events. He was screwed. Really screwed. He needed her to go away or things would get bad.

Very bad.

"Officer Lang to you," she said with a poisonous tone. She glared down at him.

Nate nodded. He shouldn't push her, but couldn't help himself. "So, how's life as a flatfoot, again?" he said. He scratched his cheek then dropped his hand to rest against the open door, positioning it closer to his pocket.

Officer Lang continued to glare at him for several moments, then said, "I'm a flatfoot because of your boss." She hitched her thumbs into her belt, the left hand next to her holstered pistol.

Nate knew the gun. A standard police-issue held fast in its holster by a leather snap-strap. He did a rough calculation on her potential speed to unsnap the weapon, draw it, and fire versus him pulling his own pistol with its long silencer from his deep pockets.

The odds came out about even.

Nate shook his head. "That's got nothing to do with me, Vicky. You know that. We're both flunkies in our respective organizations. Bottom of the ladder, as it were. Well, I make more money, of course." He smiled at her.

Officer Lang's face contorted into a scowl and Nate thought she would draw on him right then and there. He tensed.

Lang made a visible effort to relax and her left hand shifted away from her pistol. "Quite the mouth on you, Nate," she said, fixing him with her stare. "Word is you've used it to stay out of jail more than once. A regular fount of information when the squeeze is put to you." The ice claw tightened more. This bitch was trying to get him to make a move on her. She had nothing on him right now. He's just sitting here, minding is own business, but she wants him to screw up so she could... what? Arrest him? Shoot him? God knows she had reason enough.

Years earlier Victoria Lang was a homicide detective. One of the best. When her old partner retired she was assigned a new stiff, a guy named Brad Fletcher. Only problem was, Brad Fletcher was in deep with Unger and his crew. Owed him big money, too. Much to Unger's delight.

I gotta cop in my pocket, Unger used to boast. *I say dance and he dances a little jig. I say lose that evidence and evidence disappears.*

But all good things must come to an end as it did for Fletcher, who got caught trying to hide a bloody knife at a murder scene on the southside.

Fletcher was raked over the coals and broke so quickly as to not even be dignified. Then he shot himself in the head, and Victoria Lang's career got caught by the same bullet.

Her partner had been on the take and she didn't know it. You can never get that stink off you, especially as a detective. Her hate for Unger and any of his associates were legendary. Associates like Nate.

Now she was a lowly flatfoot and probably would be one for the rest of her days. Or at least until she made Nate shoot her.

Nate counted to five, then said in a calm voice. "That ain't true and you know it, Officer." He emphasized her title. "Anyone with real information, like currently active detectives, knows I don't say nuthin about nuthin." Someone shouted from the north about half a block away. Officer Lang looked, but Nate kept his eyes locked on her. What the hell game was she playing? All these accidents right nearby and she's taking time to hassle him? Had to be emotion that drove her to confront him. Pulled her away from those in direct need just to piss in his face.

Was this bitch crazy?

The pistol weighed heavy in his pocket. His hand itched for it.

Officer Lang frowned, then unhooked the radio mike on her chest. She squeezed at its button, but the device didn't make a sound. Not a squawk or hiss of static.

"Damnit," she said. "Still dead?" She pressed at it a few more times. Click-click-click.

Nate found this very interesting. "Radio not working today, Vicky? Might want to get that checked. Never know when you'll need backup to save your skinny, square ass." Officer Lang's eyes flared, but another shout drew her attention. Again, Nate thought she was about to draw her weapon. Instead, she leaned in close and pointed a finger at him. "Stay right here. I have more questions for you."

Nate shrugged and held up his hands. "No problem, Vicky. I await your return."

She glared at him, then another shout, this one for help, pulled her away. Nate watched her square ass wiggle in her uniform trousers as she hustled down the sidewalk.

He let out a sigh of relief, but now faced a dilemma.

Of course, he wouldn't just sit here and wait for little miss square ass to interrogate him, maybe even get into a shoot-out with her. Yet she could now place him in the immediate vicinity of a triple murder. Even the drunkest homicide detective would have no problem linking Perry to Unger's crew, which Nate was a known member of.

Or he could simply leave. Walk away and go to ground for a while which was standard procedure after a hit, anyway.

There were no other direct witnesses here. Too much chaos was going on. Only Victoria Lang and her broken radio could place him near the scene.

This was intriguing. Phones were dead. Cars were dead. That plane was dead.

And her radio was dead. Which meant she hadn't called Nate in. Yet.

Huh.

Nate stood and slammed the door. He turned slowly around, taking in the immediate area. Past the children in the park were a large cluster of trees. Beyond that was Greenside avenue. That would do.

He slipped on his nylon mask, withdrew his pistol and walked in the same direction Officer Lang had gone.

He found her a couple of houses down in a yard surrounded by high hedges. Lang was hunched over, giving CPR to an elderly man on the ground. An old woman, presumably the man's wife, fretted next to them.

"Maybe it's his pacemaker?" the old lady said. She turned to look at Nate walking swiftly toward them and gasped in surprise. No electricity, then a dying husband and now a masked man on her property. What next?

Officer Lang turned at the woman's gasp and her eyes widened as Nate aimed his pistol. "You shouldn't have been here," he said and shot her through the temple.

The old woman was to stunned to scream. Nate thanked her for her silence by shooting her, too.

Then, as an afterthought, he shot the old man. Nate figured he was actually doing the guy a favor, at this point.

He immediately moved to the backyard which he accessed through an open gate. He climbed over several fences and in a few minutes emerged near the park. Slipping off his mask, he walked to the trees at the rear.

His heart hammered in his chest, but the ice claw's grip had vanished.

No one screamed at him. No signs of pursuit. No direct witnesses to his presence.

Flush with the success of not one, but six murders, Nate felt like skipping along like one of the playing children.

He'd never done six before. Not all in one day, at least.

As he stepped through the trees and onto Greenside's sidewalk, he was confronted by dozens of stalled-out vehicles. Up and down the street, across four lanes, were cars, vans and trucks as far as he could see. At least eight blocks of dead metal and fiberglass. People were everywhere, confused, angry, some even crying.

This is big, he thought. But how big? How many more blocks were like this? City wide? And for how much longer? No cars, no planes, no phones, no sirens or police radios.

He felt himself getting excited at the prospects, almost to the point of being aroused.

There is opportunity in chaos. Someone important said that, but he was clueless as to whom. Maybe it was him, right now thinking it.

He looked at his phone, still dead, the screen black. Maybe this would go on for a long time.

How long would he need?

He'd turned left, to face north. His post-job instinct was to take his out – his escape route to a farm Unger controlled at the far outskirts of the city. Hole up. Stay low.

But, instead, he turned south and his feet carried him forward. Into town.

There is opportunity in chaos.

As he passed bewildered people, he smiled to himself. If Unger wanted to know if the job was finished, then Nate would tell him.

Face to face.

CHAPTER SIX

Wyatt helped Ethan carefully walk down the alleyway back to the street, trying not to let his anger show.

It was his fault his friend had been hurt. If he'd kept his mouth shut and simply gave Casket what little money they had, Ethan would not be bleeding all over the place right now.

Wyatt's temper had always been his curse and scars marred his skin to prove it. Rage issues. That's what he had. But then, didn't everyone? Avoiding alcohol was key to him not beating the ever loving crap out of anyone who got on his bad side. But alcohol was the hobo's mana, their gateway to a different reality, one where they could forget about their awful existence. And everyone Wyatt knew lived for a bottle of the stuff.

"Could really use a drink right now," Ethan said, as if reading his mind.

Wyatt chuckled. "You need a doctor. The sauce can wait."

"I need a pretty nurse. Think you can call one up and get her down here, pronto?"

"Forgot my Rolodex of hot nurse numbers, but I'll see what I can scrounge up for you, you old goat."

Once they made it to the street, Wyatt paused to look around. Cars were still parked all over the place in messed up locations, with even more people standing about. Everyone looked agitated and confused.

"What in the hell is up with everybody today?" Ethan said, looking pale. "Can't they just get their shit together and move on?"

Wyatt glanced down the street in both directions. Vehicles jammed the roadway, but none were moving. In fact, not one had its engine on that he could tell.

"You hear that?" Wyatt said.

"What? The sound of my spirit leaving my body?"

"No. The cars. They aren't even idling. They've all been turned off."

Ethan winced, again. "Screw the cars, get a damned phone!"

"Okay, but let's set you down first." He helped Ethan over to a bus stop.

A chubby teenage girl stood waiting for the bus, scowling at her smartphone. As Wyatt eased Ethan onto the stop's bench, she turned her back to them.

"Miss," Wyatt said, walking over to her. "Miss, can I please use your phone?"

She didn't respond. The girl was either completely deaf or ignoring him.

"I need to call an ambulance. My friend is hurt."

The girl whirled to face him. "My phone isn't working right now. See?" She held it up so Wyatt could see its dark screen.

Wyatt blinked with confusion. Was she messing with him? "Can you turn it on, please? My friend needs an ambulance."

"It's not off, moron," the girl scoffed. "The battery is dead or something. Expensive piece of crap." She glared at the blackened screen.

"But-," Wyatt said, before she cut him off.

"My phone is not working!" she suddenly shrieked, causing Wyatt to take a step back. "Why can't you understand that!"

"Ah, for Christ's sake," Ethan said from the bench.

Before Wyatt could ask again, the girl stepped out onto the street and looked eastward. "Where's the stupid bus? This traffic jam is screwing with my schedule!"

Scoffing in frustration, she turned away and marched down the middle of the street, navigating around stalled vehicles.

"That, there, is wife material," Ethan said, grinning weakly.

Wyatt made a herculean effort to control his temper. Every fiber of his being demanded he run after that bitch and take the phone from her. But that would only add to their dilemma.

"Try that guy," Ethan said, pointing at a man standing next to a car in the opposite lane.

"He better not be wife material," Wyatt said as he marched across the street.

At the middle of the road, he paused. Both directions appeared to be cluttered with vehicles as far as he could see. None of them were moving or running their engines. Even the street light at a nearby intersection was dead. Very strange.

But there was something else he noticed, perhaps even stranger still. The quiet. No car engines or garbage trucks in the distance. Other than the occasional shout, or profanity spewing driver, it was incredibly still, almost peaceful.

I could get use to this, Wyatt found himself thinking. But whatever oddity that had killed the cars would be fixed soon, he was sure. Good things can't last forever.

He approached the man standing next to his car, who was glancing from his phone to Wyatt.

"Hello, sir," said Wyatt. "Can you help me? I need to use your phone. My friend needs an ambulance."

The man arched an eyebrow as he glanced over at Ethan on the bench. "Ambulance? You want 911?"

"Yeah, please," Wyatt said, hopeful.

The man shook his head. "Sorry, but my phone is dead." He held it up to Wyatt. Black screen. "Funny thing is that it happened around the same time my car decided to conk out on me." He waved a hand at the other nearby vehicles. "Looks as if they all did, too."

Wyatt grew frustrated. "Okay, thanks." He looked around, trying to judge who to approach next.

The man watched Ethan. "Your friend doesn't look to good. What happened?"

Wyatt didn't want to get into it, but didn't want to be rude. "We had an altercation with a disagreeable third party."

The man nodded. "They're always disagreeable, aren't they?"

"These ones, especially," Wyatt said. The people around them weren't using their phones. Instead, they glared at their little electronic devices trying to will them to turn on. "What happened here?"

The man shrugged. "Just like I said, really. I was driving along on my way to work when the engine suddenly went completely dead and all the lights on the panel blinked off. Thank God the brakes still worked or I would have rear-ended someone." He nodded to a cluster of cars just ahead of his own. "They weren't so fortunate. Maybe it happened to them and they couldn't react in time."

Wyatt noticed the man wore a watch. "That still working?"

The man looked at it, holding it close to his face and squinted. "Nope. This, too. Damn!"

"And this just happened?"

"About twenty minutes ago, yeah."

Wyatt was completely flummoxed by it all. What the hell is going on?

"But do you know what is really troubling?" the man said.

"What?"

"Where are the police? The fire department? No one has shown up, so that means either they are completely unaware of what's happened on this street or..."

"Or they've got the same problem," Wyatt finished, not liking what he heard. He listened for a few moments. "No sirens at all."

"Nope."

So that would mean no ambulance. Maybe not for a long time. He looked over at his friend. Ethan slouched on the bench, his hand over the gauze. Even from here, Wyatt could tell he wasn't doing well.

What was he going to do with him now?

He and Ethan had been friends for years. He use to see Ethan at the weekly soup kitchen next to Saint Catherine's Church. They started chatting and eventually became good friends.

Wyatt was very protective of his dumpster diving route, but Ethan kept insisting on tagging along. "Who wants to roll around in garbage by themselves?" he had said. Turned out he was right. Having Ethan along for his morning rounds helped take the edge of the perpetual loneliness he'd gotten accustom to. As they worked, they talked a lot and about everything.

But now Ethan was in some serious trouble, possibly life threatening.

Because of me, Wyatt thought, feeling his anger grow. I should have kept my big fat mouth shut and gave those assholes our money. Then maybe my only friend in the world wouldn't be bleeding to death at a God-damned bus stop, right now.

To the man, he asked, "Hey, do you know of a hospital around here?"

"Well, I know of a private clinic some ways down north of that intersection there."

"How far?"

The man shrugged. "No clue. But I'd guess a good twenty blocks, maybe more."

Wyatt cursed inwardly. But what else could he do? Sit here and wait for this nonsense to sort itself out, hoping that an ambulance could eventually be called? Or haul Ethan's weakening ass down twenty blocks on the chance of finding a clinic that might not really be there?

A commotion broke out behind them among a cluster of dead vehicles. Some people were shoving each other around and yelling.

This is getting ugly. If people's nerves are frayed now, what will things be like in a few hours? Or a few days?

Wyatt shook his head at the prospect. He didn't need to think on other people right this moment. Only his friend mattered.

He thanked the man and trotted over to Ethan.

His friend's pallor was ashen, blood completely soaking his left side and down his trousers.

"How you doing?" Wyatt asked, trying not to look as worried as he felt.

"Just peachy," Ethan said. His whole body was limp like his joints had given up on keeping things together. "Got a medevac on route, yet?"

Wyatt chuckled. "No, no medevac." He handed Ethan the water bottle. "Here, drink this."

Ethan took it graciously and guzzled the water down.

"Actually, I'm going to be your medevac."

"Really," Ethan said, dubious. "You gonna grow blades or wings or something and whisk me away?"

"Not quite," Wyatt said. "Wait here, I'll be right back, okay?"

Ethan shrugged, a weak gesture. "Don't worry, I don't think I can crawl very far even if I wanted to."

It pained Wyatt to leave his friend alone, but he had to. Quickly, he ran down the alleyway and back to their carts.

He unlocked them, then took turns moving them around, testing their wheels. The one for glass bottles looked to be in the best shape, so he dumped it out.

Without bothering to lock the other cart, he ran back down the alley, rattling up a tremendous noise.

He pushed the cart up to Ethan and gestured at it with a smile. "Your medevac as ordered."

Ethan, despite his weakened conditions, gave the cart a doubtful look. "Really? You're gonna push me around in that?"

"Sure. Works for cans, why not for you?"

"Well, I guess I'm recyclable in the grand scheme of things." He shoved himself up off the bench with Wyatt's help.

"But where are we gonna go?" Ethan asked as he crawled unceremoniously into the cart. He flopped inside so he was facing backwards, his legs up over the sides like a mischievous kid in a shopping mall. He grunted in pain at the movement.

"To get you fixed up, buddy," Wyatt said with a smile he didn't feel.

The man from the car trotted over. "Hey, you taking him to the clinic?"

"Yeah," Wyatt said.

"Then here, take this." The man held out a fold of money bills.

Wyatt and Ethan stared in shock.

Wyatt snapped out his reverie and asked, "What's that for?"

"Unless you guys have insurance, you might have trouble getting help from the clinic. This isn't much, but it should be enough to get your friend looked at," the man said.

Wyatt stared at the proffered cash. So much of it. Several hundred, at least. "I.. I don't know.." he said with uncertainty. No one had ever given him that much cash before. A couple of bucks, sure. But hundreds of dollars? Never.

"Oh, hell, Wyatt," Ethan said. "Take the money. At the very least it can pay for my funeral."

Wyatt accepted the money graciously and shoved it inside his jacket. "Thank you. I mean it." Then, as an afterthought asked, "What's your name?"

"Ruben," the man said. "Now get him out of here."

Wyatt nodded at Ruben, again, and then pushed the cart, still in shock.

As they rattled along, Wyatt found his mind in a daze. That has to be the kindest thing anyone had ever done for him before. And for Ethan.

"See, not all people are complete shit," Wyatt said as he pushed the rattling cart down the road, navigating around vehicles.

"The jury is still out," Ethan said. His arms and legs shook with the cart's movement, all the energy gone out of him.

Wyatt looked at his friend with a mix of pity, rage and confusion. Why was this happening to them? They should be in an ambulance by now if the damned power worked.

As he pushed the cart along, he found his thoughts echoed in the conversations of the people he passed.

What in the hell was going on?

CHAPTER SEVEN

Nate

After walking ten long blocks down Greenside avenue, Nate was ready to start shooting people.

He usually avoided crowds in general. No parties, or get-togethers or baseball games. Those were for the lesser folk, the chum of the sea.

In fact, if he had to count how many friends he had on his fingers he'd come up with a fist. He didn't need friends. More of a hindrance to his line of work. Can't trust people, and you really couldn't trust the jackals in the underworld where he worked.

So having to listen to all the whining and wailing of the people he passed began to fray his already shortened nerves.

Car after car, helpless drivers stood beside them. Nearly every vehicle had bumped into the one in front of it at cruising speed. Hoods were crumpled, back lights shattered, windshields cracked. The result was one long, continuous line of vehicular mayhem in both directions.

And everybody screamed or yelled at everyone else.

"Why didn't you watch where you're going?"

"No brakes! I couldn't stop!"

"My brakes worked, but I have no power."

"My horn wouldn't even work!"

"Call your insurance company – if you can!"

"My neck!"

"My car!"

This tension added up. At one point, he came upon an eighteen wheeler which had jackknifed on the road, the driver having tried to stop, but couldn't do it fast enough. He'd plowed through cars, creating a wake of overturned vehicles, some on top of each other.

Two men were fighting amongst this carnage while others tried to stop them or looked on.

Nate paused to watch the circus, feeling his blood rise. He very much wanted to jump into the fray, show them how a beat-down is done properly. But after a few minutes, he grew bored and continued on.

A pretty girl knelt under a tree next to an older man, maybe her father. The old coot clutched at his chest, gasping heavily.

She saw Nate as he walked by and waved frantically at him. "Can you help me, please!" He found her high pitched voice cute. He walked over.

The girl looked relieved. "Oh, thank God! No one will help us. I don't know what it is. Do you know how to-," she stopped talking when Nate leaned down and scooped a cell-phone from the old man's lap.

Nate peered at its black screen, thumbing it.

"What are you doing?" the girl asked, confused and frantic. "My phone doesn't work. No one's does."

"Figures," Nate said, disappointed. He tossed the phone back onto the man's lap and walked away, the girl too stunned to say more.

Nate took out his own dead phone, not expecting a change in its status. There wasn't.

"Won't be needing this anymore," he said and threw it.

The phone ricocheted loudly off the passenger door of a souped-up red Camaro, chipping the paint and leaving a dent.

"Hey! What the hell!" screamed the driver, who had been examining the damage to his hood. The front end was firmly wedged under the rear bumper of a landscaping truck.

The driver had to climb over his windshield to confront Nate.

Nate stopped and waited.

"You're going to pay for that!" the driver screamed, waving at the dent.

Nate laughed, a deeply mocking sound. Something he practiced. "Your hood looks like that, but you get your panties in a twist over a little dent?" He sneered at the driver. "Got your priorities backwards, don't you think?"

The driver, a younger man in his twenties, had a lean muscular build. Nate could tell it was all for show and not for use. Doubted the guy could even throw a good punch.

The driver came right up to Nate and got in his face. "Who the hell do you think you are? You're gonna pay for-."

Nate's arm shot out from his side, no telegraphing at all. His fist connected with the tip of the other man's nose and kept on going, crunching cartilage.

The man's angry screams became a yelp of pain. His head snapped back, and he stumbled, knees buckling, then fell to the concrete. Blood exploded from his mashed nose.

Nate stepped forward and kicked him in the stomach. The man folded into himself, keening in pain.

"Think I should pay for it?" he said, kicking the man again.

"Okay! Okay!" the man begged, trying to block the kicks with his legs and hands.

Nate kicked again. "Piece of shit Camaro. Why don't you drive a real car?" He didn't really mean that, but was too pissed off to care.

"Stop that!" someone shouted.

Nate looked up to find a small crowd of people gathering around. A fat wide-eyed woman held up her hands. "Stop hurting him!"

The back of Nate's neck prickled and, in one fluid motion, instantly produced his pistol.

The crowd gasped in surprise.

With the silencer attachment, Nate realized that the pistol looked a little comical. He waved it at them.

"What's a matter with you idiots?" he said, almost conversationally. "Never seen a good shit-kicking before?"

Wanting it to just end, the man on the ground said, "I'm sorry! Okay? I'm sorry!"

"What?" Nate asked, aiming at him.

The man's eyes widened. Now he knew who he was really dealing with. Not some slob walking down the street, but an apex predator.

"Said I'm sorry," the man said, tears streaming down his face. Whether he cried from the pain or for his life, Nate couldn't tell.

Nate looked over the little group of frightened people. It felt strange standing before them like this without a mask on. It felt liberating. "Anyone got a working phone?" he asked.

Every head shook, no.

"Huh," Nate said, then lowered the pistol and walked away, continuing south.

This is big, he thought as he sauntered along the side of the road. Whatever's happened is bigger than he originally considered. How does someone turn everything off at once? Never mind turning things off – everything is effectively dead. Was it the Russians? Those crazy Koreans?

As he picked his way along the sidewalk, people spotted the pistol in his hand and gave him a wide birth. Nate didn't notice, so lost in thought.

This has got to be an attack of some sort. Some sort of device. A death ray, or something. Or a thing that sucks up electricity or negates it. Then he stopped, hit with a thought. Nuclear? Was it a bomb?

He slowly spun around scanning the horizon. The black column of smoke from the plane crash mottled the sky to the south, but it was joined by other columns, most smaller. He counted six rising from different locations. Fires all over. He glanced at the crush of cars on the road. And no way for firefighters to get to them, even if their fire engines were still working, which he doubted.

But he didn't see a mushroom cloud. If there was a nuclear attack, people would be really freaking out right now. Still, it didn't mean a bomb hadn't gone off nearby, or in space. He'd spent a lot of time surfing the internet and one of the factoids he learned was that nukes killed anything electrical.

He continued on, lost in thought, but slipped the pistol back in his pocket.

Vicky's radio didn't work. Cars weren't moving, and planes – at least one he knew of – were crashing. Cops were going to have one hell of a day on their hands if this was city wide, which it was starting to shape up to be.

He arrived at an intersection which was densely packed with dead vehicles. There were more people here, most looked to be workers from a huge nearby office building. The sign outside the building made him pause. Pickering Office Tower.

Well, well, he thought. That was a name from the past. Not the building, but of one of its inhabitants.

Nate felt a strange mix of anger and excitement course through his body.

There is opportunity in chaos.

He walked toward the office tower. There were clusters of office geeks talking excitedly to each other and waving their cellphones around, trying to understand the situation.

Nate approached a trio of women, all wearing long tight skirts which he found appealing. "Hey, what's going on?" he asked a pretty blonde.

The blonde was a little startled by his appearance. Nate didn't look like he worked in a cubicle by any stretch of the imagination. "Uh, the power's gone out. Can't work."

A brunette gave Nate the once over and liked what she saw. "Yeah, they might give us the rest of the day off." Her eyes flashed at him.

Nate grinned. "I think it'll be longer than that. More like a vacation, an extended one."

"Why's that?" the blonde asked, more concerned now.

Nate didn't answer. He tilted his head back to look up the tall building. "How many stories do you think that is?"

The blonde giggled nervously. "It's twenty-one stories. I should know. I had to climb down every last one of them."

"Why?" Nate asked.

She giggled nervously, again. "Because the elevators aren't working. You need electricity for that."

"Huh," Nate said. Then he asked, "Isn't there a law office up there?"

The blonde blinked in surprise. "Yes, Anderson and Associates. That's where I work. Did you have an appointment?" He was starting to make them nervous.

"Yeah," Nate said, "I got an appointment with Jonas Anderson. He out here somewhere?" He looked around at the crowd.

The blonde shook her head. "No, he's waiting it out in his office. It would take more than a power outage to get Mr. Anderson out of there on a work day."

Nate said, "We'll see about that." He left the perplexed women and headed to the front doors.

"But the elevators don't work!" the blonde called after him.

He entered the main foyer which was crowded with people. Others trickled through the doors, heading outside. Everyone was annoyingly excited at this curious event, so dull were their lives.

Nate found the building registry on a wall and scanned the names.

Anderson & Associates – Partners in Law - 21st Floor.

Figures it would be the top damn floor. He shrugged. Guess he had to work for this. Besides, it was the least he could do for Chris.

He found the stairs and started up. Tired looking fat men in shirts and ties bumbled downward. It was dark, but each floor had propped open the stairwell door, letting some sunlight in from the floor's windows.

At the tenth floor, Nate found a maintenance man up on a low ladder. He was fiddling with an emergency light which was wedged up in a corner.

"Shouldn't those be working?" Nate asked. He'd passed one on each level, all off.

"Should, yeah," the man said. "But something is wrong with the batteries." He tapped the large narrow block beneath the light. "Should have switched over to them the second the power went out."

"The batteries don't work, either?"

The man nodded in the gloom. "Not just these, but all of them." He held out a large flashlight and flicked its switch back and forth. Nothing happened. "Phones are toast, too."

"Huh," Nate said, and left the man to his futile efforts. But before he climbed a couple of steps he turned back and asked, "What do you think could do that? Cause a power outage and kill the batteries?"

The maintenance man gave it a moment of thought, then said, "Aliens," and returned to his work.

For the next eleven floors Nate played that word over and over in his mind. Aliens. That can't be. Could it? An alien attack?

As he finally reached the twenty-first floor, he pushed the thought of an alien invasion out of his mind. He'd think on that later. For now, time to catch up with an old friend.

He left the stairwell and entered a lush office foyer, the kind only lawyer money could buy. There wasn't a receptionist at the desk so he went exploring.

After passing empty cubicles and offices, he heard voices coming from an open door marked Board Room.

Inside, he found two men pouring over stacks of papers and giant law books. A pair of laptops sat on the huge table, their screens black.

The men looked up as Nate entered. One of them, a fat man with a stylish goatee and powder-blue tie, gasped.

"What's up, Jonas?" Nate asked the fat man. "Long time, no see."

Jonas stood in alarm as Nate walked up to him. "N-Nate! Oh, what a surprise. I wasn't expecting you."

"You weren't expecting me?" Nate said, his voice rising with anger. "Jonas, you should always be expecting me." He pulled out his pistol, but kept it by his side.

"Oh, God!" Jonas said, raising his hands. His fat blubber quivered beneath his expensive clothes. Clothes Nate helped pay for.

Nate grabbed Jonas by his powder-blue tie. "You should have been expecting me every single day since Chris died. Which wouldn't have happened if you did your damned job!"

The other lawyer, tall and skinny with glasses, had stood up. He backed up against the wall, eyes wide with terror.

Jonas was beside himself with fear. "But it wasn't me! It was the judge. You know the evidence was too strong."

"Too strong?!" Nate screamed, spitting his words over the man's face. "I paid you all that money so the evidence wouldn't matter!"

"B-but they had Chris on video, pulling the trigger! You saw it yourself!"

Nate breathed heavily, his rage growing hotter by the second. "You know they shanked him, right? He bled out in the showers!" He pressed his face up against the terrified lawyer's and screamed, "But before they shanked him, they took turns fucking him in the ass!" Nate's eyes were wide, crazed. "He wouldn't have been there if you did your fucking job!"

The skinny guy with glasses suddenly ran to the door, his tie flapping about. Nate calmly aimed and shot the fleeing man in the head, splattering blood and bits of brain matter over a large beautiful painting of a sailboat.

Jonas cried out in shock then grabbed at his chest in pain.

Nate looked at him in disgust. "Oh, no. You don't get to die on me before I can kill you." He aimed at one of the nearest windows which lined one wall of the huge room. Six shots punctured the reinforced glass, creating a large cluster of cracks.

Nate heaved the sagging man to his feet. "You got some co-workers downstairs who want to see you, Jonas."

Jonas gasped in pain, eyes locked onto the shattered window. He shit his pants.

With his free hand, Nate pulled the lawyer along by his tie and hurled him at the window.

"Nooooo!" Jonas screamed, then smashed through the glass and vanished from sight.

Nate peered out the window and watched the fat man plummet. He'd never seen someone fall from this high up, before.

Jonas hit the pavement below, narrowly missing groups of office workers. The lawyer didn't so much as splatter as he practically turned inside out with the impact.

As Nate reentered the stairwell and began the long descent, he found one thought playing over and over in his mind.

Aliens. Now wouldn't that be a sight?

CHAPTER EIGHT

Wyatt

The streets were complete chaos.

That would be the best way Wyatt could describe them. Pushing the cart with Ethan's weight wasn't a problem. He'd been pushing carts for years. Despite his lifestyle, he ate okay, thanks to soup kitchens and grocery store refuse. He was in fairly good health.

But trying to navigate the streets with all its cars, trucks, and tractor trailers was really getting to him. It was like God dumped all these vehicles in his way to create an obstacle course. To test his resolve. How badly do you want to save your friend, Wyatt? Do you think it will make up for all those things you've done?

By Wyatt's estimation, they had traveled eight blocks in the last two hours. All of it level ground for which he was grateful. But the crowds of people sitting and standing on the sidewalks stopped him dead in his tracks many times.

Attempting to use the road itself had become nearly impossible. As a major thoroughfare, the morning rush hour had been in full swing when everything went dead. Many drivers managed to stop, but others didn't. A chain reaction backed up against another chain reaction. The result was six lanes of vehicular carnage.

The view of so many dead vehicles lined from horizon to horizon reminded Wyatt of those horror movies where the world was ending. People fleeing the city from malevolent aliens, or city crushing monsters, or invading armies. Only none of those scenarios were the case here, but Wyatt would welcome any one of them right now.

He was getting close to losing his temper. But he kept on pushing through. He had to.

Ethan jiggled in the cart, eyes half closed.

"You still with me, buddy?" Wyatt asked, as he wiped a thick sheen of sweat from his face.

"Yup," Ethan said, perking up. "Not going anywhere you ain't taking me." He looked about at the cars and people they slowly cruised by. "Damn, someone really screwed up somewhere didn't they?"

"How's that?" Wyatt asked. He needed to keep Ethan awake and talking.

"Well, the way I see it maybe the government discovered something they shouldn't have, and this is the end result."

"Like a bomb?"

"Sure, a bomb, or a device or something meant to knock out the Russians. Only we got hit with it, instead. I mean, look around. Have you ever seen anything like this before in all your days? I sure haven't."

"I'm certain you've seen a lot considering you're older than dirt. But no, I've never seen this before."

Ethan thought for a moment. "Maybe the sun did it."

"Okay, the blood loss is making you a little delusional. You've gone from bombs for Russians, to the sun. Bit of a stretch?" Wyatt said, teasing.

Ethan shook his head, weakly. "Not at all. Can happen. Oh, hell, it has happened for all we know. Solar flares or sunspots or whatever. Could be that the sun burped and a big ass wave of radiation hit the Earth and knocked out everything electrical."

Wyatt thought on this a few moments as he swerved the cart around a fat man who stood unmoving in the middle of the sidewalk.

As Wyatt gave the guy a dirty look, he said to Ethan, "Okay, that might make some sense. But I've never heard of this happening before, like ever."

"Oh, it's happened," Ethan said as he tried to adjust his position. It wasn't the most comfortable way to sit, especially if you've been stabbed. "Back in the eighteen-eighties or so a bunch of telegraph wires fried out. There wasn't much electrical back then, but what little there was got sizzled."

"Like sparks and stuff?"

"Yeah."

Wyatt gazed up at the endless lines of wires which extended from the telephone poles along the road. "Doesn't look fried to me. Everything looks the same, except for all these damned people and dead cars."

"Yeah. I dunno about that. Maybe it wasn't the sun. Just a theory."

"But a good one. Better than my theory, by a long way."

"You have a theory, do you, Einstein?"

"Yup."

"Well, enlighten me, please."

Wyatt stopped. The tiredness seeped through his bones and joints.

Ethan frowned at him. "Whoa, junior. I think you've overexerted yourself. Take a break. Here, drink some water."

Wyatt accepted the bottle and took a long swig. His chatting was masking the mounting frustration he felt. "Where is the God-damned clinic?"

He slowly spun around trying to make out all the signs for the different offices and strip malls around them. He'd been checking as they traveled, but nothing close to resembling a clinic presented itself.

Beside them, a family sat in a minivan, its side door open. He could hear everyone complaining inside, bewildered at their situation. By this time, nearly everybody he'd seen had completely given up on their phones and took to interrogating the other stranded people closest to them. Have they heard anything? Did they know what was going on? When would help arrive?

With the moronic conversations, and the heat, and the need to get Ethan some help, the tension inside him was building up.

He was afraid it wouldn't take much to make him blow.

"Yo, Einstein," Ethan barked.

Wyatt snapped out his thoughts. "What? What is it?"

"Lost you there for a second. You were going to enlighten me?"

"Right, sorry," Wyatt said, and handed the bottle back. He resumed pushing the cart. The beginning of the next block was a short distance ahead. Maybe the clinic was there. "My theory is this. I think God finally got fed up with how the world had gone and screwed itself and decided to do a reset."

"A reset?"

"Yeah, what better way to get people to pull their heads out of their collective asses than to take away what was most important to them?"

"Electricity?"

Wyatt nodded. "Sure. But maybe it's more than that. Take away all the electricity and what do you got left?"

"The mother of all traffic jams," Ethan offered.

"Yup, that's one thing. But what does that represent? It's not just this traffic jam, but the fact that all the cars and buses and stuff no longer work. What happens when they never start up again?"

"A lot of people will have to walk to work," Ethan said. "Would do them good. Hell, you and I do that every damn day!"

"Yeah, a lot of walking. But where would they be walking to? If they go to the office, and the computers and machines no longer even turn on, what do they do then?"

Ethan looked pensive. "Start dumpster diving?"

Wyatt laughed, something he hadn't done for several long hours. "Well, they could, but where would those cans come from? Need machines to make the cans."

"And trucks to deliver the cans to the store," Ethan said. "Hell, they couldn't even dig the aluminum from the ground to feed into their dead can-making machines."

They passed a bus who's passengers now loitered on the grass next to the sidewalk. Hardly anyone gave the two of them a look, so caught up in their own dilemma. Wyatt was used to being ignored all the time. But he found a strange satisfaction in seeing these people totally flummoxed to the point of being helpless. Now he was the one making progress, and they were to be ignored.

Ethan said, "So, no more cans for us?"

Wyatt shook his head. "I don't know, partner. All I do know is if this doesn't fix itself right quick, things are going to get like the Lord of the Flies."

"Like a bunch of kids on an island?"

"Like no technology. What if one of these saps get mugged, how they going to call the police? What if there's a murder? No cameras around, no phones, no nothing that would normally make someone think twice before committing a crime."

This thought made Ethan look more pale. "Sheesh, now that is messed up, right there."

"Okay, back to the cans in the store," Wyatt said.

"Or not being there any longer."

"But say there still is. How do you buy it?"

"Money."

"Yeah, but what money? Everything is electronic. Pay from a debit card or credit card. Can't do that without the juice flowing through those lines overhead. Now, you and I are old school. Everything is cold, hard cash with us."

"If we had any."

"True, but I'll bet that you and I have more hard currency on us than anyone on this street. They all got cards linked to their bank accounts, which is online. Or was."

"Shit," Ethan said, true realization dawning on him. As they passed more stranded people he looked at them with an odd expression.

"What are you thinking now?" Wyatt asked.

"I'm thinking these folks are absolutely screwed. Lord of the Flies is right. You nailed that bang on. But do you really think this will go on for much longer? Can't someone fix this?"

Wyatt shrugged. "To be honest, I don't really care. Right now I just need to get you some help. Electricity or no electricity."

They rattled down the sidewalk for a while, both men lost in thought.

"I just realized something," Ethan said.

"Now it's your turn to enlighten me, you old goat."

"There hasn't been a news or police chopper flying overhead this whole time."

"No, you're right. I ain't seen or heard one at all."

"I figure the police would be watching from overhead by now. If they could."

"If they could."

"So, if choppers and planes can't take off anymore, what happened to all the ones that were in the sky at the time this occurred?"

Wyatt paused and the rattling mercifully stopped. "God damn, that is one scary thought."

They both looked up at the sky as if expecting to find a plane descending upon them.

"Jesus," Ethan said. "Guess Baldy did see something. How many planes are in the sky at any one time?"

"Well, we got the airport, so that means lots of air traffic. I don't know. Lots. But even one plane in the sky is one too many when their power fails."

"And what if this crap has affected the entire country? Hell, the whole world?"

Wyatt shook his head. "I don't even want to think about that. Too terrifying to contemplate." Then he spotted something further ahead.

"What," Ethan said, seeing his expression. "What is it now?"

A grin spread across Wyatt's face and his eyes lit up.

In the distance, he saw the one thing he needed to find right at that moment.

An ambulance.

CHAPTER NINE

Despite wearing boots and a long jacket, Nate rode the mountain bike like he was born to it.

At a guess, it had been seven or eight years since he'd ridden anything with two wheels that didn't have a motor.

He sped down the street, navigating around accidents and dead vehicles. The only real obstacles were people, but those he just yelled at and they quickly scampered out of his way.

Unger's unscheduled check-in would have to wait a little while longer. First, Nate needed to make a pit-stop and freshen up. Gotta look good for the boss.

Through a maze of avenues and cross-streets, he arrived at a squat house perched close to the road. It was of ancient design, compact and square.

An old hippy woman sat on the front stoop, smoking a joint. As Nate rode up, she looked him over and raised her eyebrows in surprise. "Nice bike, Nate. Where'd ya get it?"

Nate stopped and got off the bike. The seat was a little low, he'd adjust it later. "Stranger gave it to me."

The eyebrows stayed up. "Gave it to you? How come?"

Nate leaned his new acquisition against the side of the stairs and shrugged. "He didn't have much of a choice."

The eyebrows dropped, and the woman resumed smoking, the conversation all but forgotten. Nate sat down next to her.

"Mind if I partake?" he asked.

The woman coughed a laugh and passed the joint over. "When have you ever not?"

Nate took a long drag, letting himself relax. It had been a stressful morning. He needed this.

The street was quiet, almost death-like. Usually, cars used this avenue to move between the major roads at either end. But not now. Maybe never again.

Returning the joint, Nate said, "How has your morning been, Crystal? Any planes drop out of the sky?"

Crystal sat back against the stairs, smoke forming wisps around her face and trailing through her long gray hair. "Nah, nothing like that." She thought on the question a moment then turned her sleepy eyes to Nate. "Why?"

Nate laughed at her confusion. Crystal hardly got riled up about anything. The world could end and she'd still be sitting right here on her stoop, smoking or chatting with the neighbors like it was the only business worth getting up to.

And maybe the world was ending.

Unperturbed by his manner, Crystal looked up at the sky, lost in idle thought. It was a pose you could almost always find her in.

He said, "You have no idea what's going on out there, do you?"

"Out where?"

He pointed toward the street and waved his arm. "There, out there in the world. You don't know what's happening."

Crystal shrugged. "Sure I know."

"What then?"

"A bunch of convoluted crap, that's what. Just only a little different than yesterday, but still shitty as always."

Nate laughed. "Yeah, I guess you're right." Perhaps in more ways than she knew.

Crystal said, "Doesn't matter what happens out there as long as I got this right here." She took another drag.

Nate laughed as he stood and headed toward the side of the house.

"Hey, why are you here so early in the day?" she said.

"Finished a job early," Nate said with a mischievous grin.

"Dare I ask?" she said.

"Nope!" Nate walked down the side of the little house and entered the backyard through a gate. Overgrowth and weeds choked up every square inch of the back of the property. The high fence, coupled with the entanglement of small trees and other foliage, blocked the view of any neighbors who might peer over.

And that was one reason why Nate had chosen this place.

The back door to the basement had a huge padlock on its latch. Nate fished out his keys and opened it.

Once inside, he closed the door. Darkness greeted him. For kicks he tried the light switch. Nothing.

He carefully moved over to the only window and yanked the curtains open. While doing so, he knocked over old cans, and piles of paper from a table.

Muted sunlight filtered in through the grimy window. He'd never opened those curtains since he started to rent this place from Crystal. Couldn't risk anyone looking in.

The room was at the ass-end of a typical basement, unfurnished save for a single plastic chair and lined with several old work tables. Boxes full of Crystal's crap were jammed into every available spot. The old hippy was a pack-rat. Anyone having to sort through this stuff would have an aneurysm just from considering it.

Perfect for hiding things in.

Nate moved a table away from one wall, then removed a piece of paneling, revealing a small crawl space. From it, he yanked out a large black dufflebag and dumped it on the table.

Inside were guns and rifles. He ran his hand over the neat pile of gleaming dark metal. God, he loved these things.

He took the pistol out of his pocket and placed it on the table. Normally he would have dumped it by now, but he had a hunch that forensics was quite possibly a thing of the past. Besides, the gun was too nice to get rid of. Worth the risk keeping it.

He selected a shotgun and a box of rounds, then sat on the little plastic chair which squeaked in protest. One by one, he fed rounds into the shotgun.

This was not his home. There wasn't a cot or sleeping bag here, nor had he ever intended this to be a place to hang out for more than a couple of hours. The less time spent with all this illegal weaponry, the better.

Crystal didn't care, which was what he paid her rent for. Initially, he kept his distance, but her casual manner and cavalier approach to things drew him into conversations with the old hippy. Over the years, they became acquaintances, of a sort. Nate would even venture to say she was a kind of sister to him.

Nate did have sisters, three of them. But two were dead, one by suicide, the other by overdose. The third was in prison down on the coast for fraud. He never spoke to her, nor her him. They both preferred it that way, which suited Nate just fine. Family was something that could be used against you. You could try to convince yourself that the scumbags you worked with or worked for would never mess with your family. But at some point, they're eventually brought into the equation, especially in a dispute.

Partly because of this, he didn't have an apartment or house. He preferred hotel rooms or staying at one of his girlfriends, of which there were many he could choose from. Can't stay in one place for too long, not in his line of work. If he needed to clean up, or a change of clothes he'd stop by one of the girls' places for a shower and a shag. One didn't have to happen before the other.

As he loaded the weapon, an image of Jonas, the fat lawyer, pinwheeling down the side of the building played through his mind. It made him smile. Chris would have approved. You weren't suppose to touch lawyers, especially your own. But Chris getting thrown in prison for life was unacceptable to Nate. Someone had to answer for it, and all other participants in that job, like the defense attorney. Irrefutable evidence or not, Chris should have walked out of that courtroom and into the nearest bar.

Didn't happen, so Jonas got himself turned inside out. Such an action would normally have serious ramifications for Nate. Possibly fatal. But he was hedging his bets it wouldn't come to that.

In fact, he was betting a lot of things were about to change for the better.

He finished the rest of his preparations and left Crystal's basement, locking the door behind him.

In the front driveway was a black Trans Am, with a dull red firebird painted across its hood. He walked past it.

"Aren't you gonna take the Bird?" asked Crystal. "Or are you on some kind of health kick now?"

"Doesn't work," Nate said as he got on his bike.

"Did you break it or something?"

"Not me."

"Well, who did then?"

"Aliens," he said with a grin and rode off. It was time he checked in with Unger.

CHAPTER TEN

Wyatt

"Buddy," Wyatt said, a wide grin spreading across his face. "I see some help for you, right up ahead."

Ethan tried to turn and look, but couldn't. "What? Some sexy asian girls dying to get their hands on this old body of mine?"

Wyatt chuckled. "Even better than that."

The ambulance was right smack dab in the middle of a crowded intersection. Dozens of vehicles surrounded it. Its lights weren't flashing and Wyatt didn't see any medics in the front cab.

Wyatt shoved at the cart, accelerating it down the sidewalk. "Let's get you over there."

At the corner of the intersection, Wyatt found he couldn't get the cart down onto the street's pavement. All the vehicles were bumper to bumper creating an impassible wall of fiberglass and steel.

Wyatt grumbled a curse and waved at the ambulance. There were still no medics that he could see.

"You're making a spectacle of yourself," Ethan said, eyes half-lidded and looking paler. "Damned attention whore."

Frustrated, Wyatt said, "Wait here, buddy. I'll get you some help." He left Ethan in the cart and stepped onto the street. A sedan blocked his way, with both ends crammed up against other vehicles, so he heaved himself onto its hood.

"Hey!" shouted the driver, a wild-eyed man with a beard. "What the hell you doing to my car?"

"It's blocking progress!" Wyatt said, sliding over it and off the opposite side. He then navigated through several rows of dead traffic this way, annoying drivers who were already very ticked off at their predicament.

So elated at the sight of the ambulance, Wyatt barely registered their complaints, nor did he shout back at them all that much. Which he considered was lucky for them.

Finally, he stepped up to the ambulance and pressed his face against its windshield. No one there.

"Ah, come on!" he said as he hurried around to the back.

He found the doors closed and when he tried to open them, they were locked.

"God damnit!" Wyatt said, banging loudly on the door.

"They're gone," said a woman standing next to a Mazda.

"Gone?" Wyatt whirled on her. "What do you mean gone?"

The woman took a step back, looking concerned. "Yeah, they left about ten minutes ago."

Wyatt turned and punched at the ambulance's doors. "This can't be happening! Why is this happening?" He thought of Ethan bleeding out and dying in the cart on the side of the road. The ambulance was right here!

The woman said, "They were transporting a patient when everything stopped. Then they hauled him over these cars, put him in a wheelchair and took off."

"Where?" Wyatt said, his anger in full bloom.

"They're too far from the hospital so I think they were going to try to get the guy to the clinic."

"Which clinic?"

"Elmdale, I think it's called. About four blocks that way," she said, pointing.

Wyatt looked in the direction, but saw only a sea of trapped vehicles, the sun glinting off them.

By now, his anger boiled. Why did they leave? If they stayed by the damned ambulance, Ethan would be getting help right now.

Wyatt ran to the front of the ambulance again and tried the doors. Locked. He looked back over the cars at Ethan, who appeared asleep, slumped in the cart.

"Damnit," Wyatt said, then returned the same route he had come, crawling over hoods and matching angry shouts with their drivers.

He reached the sidewalk, again, and stood sweating profusely next to Ethan. "How you doing, buddy?"

Ethan smiled weakly. "Haven't taken to the ghost, yet, if that's what you're wondering." He didn't look good at all. "The medics there?"

Wyatt shook his head. His heart was racing in his chest. "No. They left with a patient. But the good news is we're close to that clinic."

"Yay," Ethan quietly cheered.

Wyatt looked at the intersection again. He needed to get Ethan over to the other side. But there was no physical way to push the cart through. He could try to go further up the street in hopes of finding a clear path across, but looking in that direction told him it would be more of the same.

"Hey, Wyatt," Ethan said.

Wyatt turned his glare toward him, his eyes frantic. "Yeah?"

"You need to relax a little. Can't have you popping on me." Ethan looked concerned. He'd seen Wyatt lose his temper before and it had never been pretty.

Wyatt barely registered the words, instead he went back to looking for a path across. If he couldn't get both Ethan and the cart across at the same time, then the only alternative was to take each one in turn. Ethan was the heaviest, so he'd take him first. If Wyatt ran out of juice by the time he got them to the other side, he'd forget about retrieving the cart.

He blinked sweat from his eyes and wiped at his face. This was a crazy idea, but any sane options were no longer on the table.

"Okay, buddy, we need to get you out of there," Wyatt said. He reached down and grabbed Ethan by an arm.

"Out?" Ethan said, but didn't resist. He let Wyatt pull him from the cart.

"Yeah, we got to cross somehow. The clinic is further down the road that way."

Ethan gazed about amused at the sight of so many vehicles rendered useless. "Maybe if we pushed the cross-walk button that would help."

Wyatt was to agitated to even hear the joke. "We can't go around so we're going over them."

"Hate to put a dent in your plan, Wyatt, but I'm as useful as a sack of shit, right now. I might fall asleep halfway."

Putting his friend's arm around his shoulder, Wyatt said, "If you fall asleep, I'll carry you. No matter what."

They stepped up to the sedan he'd crossed over twice before. The wild-eyed driver stood next to it, glaring at them with open hostility. "What do you think you're going to do now, huh?" he said.

"Saving my friend, if you don't mind," Wyatt said, and helped Ethan up onto the hood.

"Now wait a minute!" yelled the driver and came up to them.

In an instant, Wyatt had the brass knuckles on and cocked his fist back.

The driver stopped with his hands up. "Whoa, easy now. No need for that." He looked at the knuckles with apprehension.

Wyatt glared at him, daring him to try something.

Ethan half-crawled, half-slid across the sedan's hood, leaving a trail of blood. He eased off onto his feet at the other side.

Ignoring the driver, Wyatt jumped onto the hood and walked across it, then dropped down.

"You did great, buddy," Wyatt said, hoisting him up again. "We got a few more to go."

"I'd say this is kinda of fun if I wasn't dying."

Wyatt took him over to the next vehicle that had a profile low enough for them to cross. It was an old style Cadillac, its hood practically an acre of metal.

As they both slid and crawled across the sun warmed hood, Ethan saw a woman staring at them with horror from the driver's seat. "Sorry I got blood on your car, lady," Ethan said, and then slid off the other side and flopped to the ground.

Wyatt hurried over to lean down next to him. "You okay? Did you hurt yourself?"

"Just my ego," Ethan said. "It was too big to begin with."

The next car crossing got them to the ambulance, right in the center of the intersection.

Wyatt and Ethan stopped to lean against it, panting and sweating.

Ethan patted the ambulance weakly. "Look, we made it."

"This isn't our stop. We're going to the clinic." It may be the only way to save your life, Wyatt thought.

"Oh, we forgot the water bottle," Ethan said.

"No, I got it right here. Don't you worry," Wyatt said, fishing the bottle out of his backpack. There was barely a finger full at the bottom.

He helped Ethan put it to his lips.

"This is a very odd situation, don't you think?" Ethan said when he finished drinking.

Wyatt looked around them. They were in the middle of an intersection surrounded by a sea of cars. Not a place he ever expected to find himself in. "Yeah, this is pretty damned odd. No argument there."

The people nearby looked despondent. Each one at a compete loss as to what to do. Leave their cars here? Go home? Go to work? Go crazy?

Wyatt tried to feel bad for them, but that lasted all of two seconds. "Screw 'em," he said, his temper still pulsing hot in his head. "What good are they, anyhow? No one is even trying to help."

"Hey, now," Ethan said. "You know I'd join you in that world hating chorus, but that guy did help us."

"What guy?"

"The guy back there, the one who gave you that wad of cash."

"Oh, right," Wyatt shook his head. "Man, things must really be bad if we've switched roles."

"Roles?"

"Now I'm cynical about people and you're not."

Ethan offered a feeble laugh. "Must be the end of the world."

Wyatt stood. "Okay, we need to get the rest of the way before we melt out here." He tugged at Ethan's arms.

Ethan tried to protest, but he no longer had the strength.

Over the next ten minutes, they crossed the other lanes of dead traffic. No one protested or put up a fuss. Either they didn't want to mess with the angry blood-covered hobo, or they didn't care.

Finally, they slid off the last hood and made it to the other sidewalk. Wyatt guided Ethan over to the only bit of empty shade under a tree not occupied and eased him to the ground.

Ethan was exhausted and horrifically pale.

Wyatt, gasping for breath and tired beyond reason, was about to sit down next to him for a brief rest. Then he had a good look at Ethan's complexion.

"Your friend doesn't look too good," a man sitting nearby said.

Wyatt gently slapped at Ethan's face, trying to get him to open his eyes. "Wake up, buddy. No time to be sleeping on the job. We're almost there."

He shook Ethan and kept slapping lightly at his face. Ethan only groaned.

"Shit," Wyatt said, and stood. With surprising strength, he pulled Ethan up onto his feet, then put him over his shoulder in a fireman's carry.

Ethan was heavy, but it was manageable. Having a body draped over his shoulder brought back memories of a darker time. He shoved them aside and focused at the task at hand.

He moved as quickly as he could down the sidewalk, barking at people to get out of his way.

Fear clutched his heart. This wasn't good. Not good at all. He had to get Ethan to the clinic and fast.

CHAPTER ELEVEN

Nate

Getting across the city was a major chore by car, let alone on a bicycle. By late afternoon, Nate had made it through two districts and only by avoiding the major roadways completely.

The highways were chaotic death-traps filled with thousands of vehicles and people. He'd considered riding up along the sides, avoiding the carnage in the middle. But just looking at all that craziness made Nate shiver. Let those idiots sort it out amongst themselves. He wouldn't go near it.

Which meant he had to travel by side-roads and these were little better than the highways.

He rode up on a shopping mall. Here the vehicles had reason to be parked, but that didn't mean the people couldn't loiter about in confusion. With no more air-conditioning, folks left the mall in droves and formed huge crowds outside the entrances. It was like a rock concert without the music. Never mind the highways, that was real chaos.

The streets around the mall were just as jammed as the parking lot. Nate kept to the opposite side of the street and managed to pass by. He pulled off down a lane and looked for a particular apartment building.

When he found it, he spotted a young punk outside, sitting in the shade of a tree. Nate rode up.

"Hey, man," Nate said as he stopped in front of him. "How they hanging?"

The punk's eyes widened slightly at Nate, but then kept his face neutral. "Oh, hey, Nate. They're hanging low and large. You?"

Nate got off his bike and propped it up against the tree. "Same," he said and looked around.

This was a residential area made of low income apartments. Because of the lack of power, people had taken to standing on their tiny balconies or out on the street in whatever shade they could find.

He asked the punk, "What's your name again?"

"David," he said, showing no offense at not being remembered. "But peeps call me Dee."

"Peeps, huh?" Nate said with a grin. "Who's crew do you run with?"

Dee scratched his chin, and Nate spotted a small pistol cinched in his waistband under his shirt. "I was with Caleb for a while, but now I'm with Granger." He didn't sound thrilled about the change in management.

"Granger, right," Nate said. "He kicking around?"

Dee considered the question for a moment, weighing which answer would get him in the least amount of trouble. Looking at Nate, the decision was easy. "Yeah, he's up on the fourth, room 412."

As Nate turned away, Dee held up a dead cell phone. "Hey, you know what the hell's going on? It's like nothing works now."

"I heard it was the aliens," Nate said, and walked to the apartment building.

The front entrance door was propped open to prevent people from breaking its glass because the buzzer system didn't work. He cruised in and found the stairs.

Nobody had bothered to prop open the stairway doors, so he was enveloped in complete darkness. He kept his hand on the rail as he slowly ascended, counting the floors.

On the fourth floor, he walked down the murky hall looking at room numbers. He heard conversations through doors and someone having what sounded like an orgy behind door 406. Maybe he'd join in later.

He stopped at 412 and waited.

There were no sounds from within, but that didn't mean anything. It was possible Granger might have spotted him outside talking to Dee, and fled. There was only one way to find out.

He checked the doorknob and was not surprised to find it unlocked. With a push, it opened wide.

Inside, he found a man sitting at a kitchen table next to a window. He had been blowing cigarette smoke outside when Nate entered and coughed.

"Granger!" Nate said with a jovial smile. "Catch you at a bad time?" He closed the door behind him while keeping his gaze on the other man.

"Oh, Nate," Granger said, sputtering around the words. His face was long and thin, with a hooked nose. Straggly hair hung down past his bony shoulders.

Granger looked like he couldn't decide whether he should stand up or stay sitting. But with Nate blocking the door, there was nowhere to run, so he remained seated.

"Came to see how things were going with you and your new wife," Nate said. He pulled out a chair from the table and sat down, positioning himself so he could move freely. "Didn't get an invite to the wedding."

Granger looked confused. "I ain't married. Not, yet anyway. We're just common law for now."

"Ah," Nate said. "I must have heard it wrong." He glanced down the little hallway that led to a couple of closed bedroom doors. "She here?"

Granger sat up and placed his elbows on the table, pretended to fiddle with his cigarette pack. "Nah, Peggy went to the store. Buy some lottery tickets and beer."

"Lottery tickets and beer?" Nate said with a laugh. "Looking to get drunk and lucky, huh?"

Granger's laugh was a little forced. "Yeah, yeah. Drunk and lucky that's a good one." His laughter trailed off.

Wanting to play this out a little longer, Nate looked over at the huge tv against the far wall. It appeared to be the same kind that Perry had which made Nate chuckle. Do all idiots shop at the same stores?

"Your power's out too, huh?" Nate asked, hitching a thumb at the tv, its screen black.

"Yeah, no power. It's been out for a while now. Haven't heard when the bastards are going to get it going again."

Nate nodded and grinned at him. He found it amusing that this human skidmark hadn't gotten the sack to ask why he was there. For long moments, he simply grinned at the other man.

Granger, already sweating from the heat, started to sweat even more. "Uh, you want a cig?" he held out the pack.

"No," Nate said. "But thank you for asking." He stared some more.

Granger leaned forward and started to speak, but Nate talked over him.

"What happened to Caleb?" Nate asked.

"Caleb?" Granger said, incredulous. One of the rules of the underworld was not to speak of the dead. Especially if they had been taken out by their own crew. Everyone knew what happened, but was forbidden to speak of it.

Granger held his hands up in confusion. "Uh, I thought you knew."

Nate continued to stare. "No, Granger. I don't know. So, why don't you tell me? Please."

Granger's hands started to tremble. To cover it, he stubbed his cigarette out in an ashtray shaped like a giant seashell. "Look, Nate, this is something Unger made clear we shouldn't-."

"Oh, I'm sure Unger made things clear to you," Nate interrupted, his voice rising. "He made it clear you would be taking over. But I want you to tell me why Caleb was removed."

Caleb had been climbing the ranks of Unger's crew, managing gambling and drugs for this section of territory. Made serious bank, too. But it wasn't enough for Unger, who expected more from his under-boss. Granger, who was beneath Caleb in rank, caught wind of this and used Unger's greed to move up. He told Unger that Caleb had been skimming this whole time, and that was why the money wasn't as good as it could be.

And as these things happened in the underworld, even an unsubstantiated rumor can get you killed. Especially if your boss is a paranoid psychopath.

This kind of inner organization Darwinism rarely caught Nate's interest. He was semi-independent which worked for both him and Unger. But this little episode had become of keen interest to Nate.

Caleb had been Chris's younger brother.

Granger stared wide-eyed at Nate, totally bewildered at the conversation. "You know I can't talk about it, Nate. You know that."

"Yeah, I know," Nate said, now seething with pent up rage. "I know why Caleb was removed. You and your fat-cow of a girlfriend put the finger on him!"

"No! That's not how it was, Nate!" Granger was pleading now, hands up in front of him. "Talk to Unger! Just talk to Unger!"

"Oh, Unger and I are going to talk, that is guaranteed," Nate shouted. "But you and I are going to finish our conversation." He had enough of this little game and stood, kicking the chair back. "Tell me you did it and I'll make this quick."

He began to pull out his pistol when the bedroom door to his right suddenly flew open.

A large fat woman roared out of the doorway with a shotgun in both hands.

Nate turned, but the pistol caught in his pocket's lining. He jumped in Granger's direction, hoping the madwoman wouldn't risk hitting her man.

He was wrong.

The shotgun blast tore a hole in the kitchen wall and effectively deafened everyone in the room.

Nate crashed into Granger, who tried to stand up. Both men fell to the floor. Nate landed directly onto Granger who gasped in pain.

Nate managed to pull his pistol free, its silencer having been removed back at Crystal's. He aimed at the fat woman, who'd racked a new round in the shotgun's chamber.

"Get out of the way, honey!" Peggy hollered.

Nate aimed at Peggy, but Granger recovered and grabbed Nate's arm with both hands. They both rolled on the ground, fighting for control of the weapon.

"Honey, get out of the way!" Peggy screamed. She kept the shotgun pointed in their direction, finger on the trigger.

"I can't..." Granger said through gritted teeth.

Nate was amazed at the skinny man's strength. He was having a hell of a time getting him off.

"God dammit GeeGee!" Peggy screamed. "Move the hell out of the-."

She didn't get to finish.

With Granger glued to his back, Nate rolled over to his side, pinning one of the skinny man's elbows under his weight. Granger gasped in pain and one hand let go of the pistol.

Their body tangle didn't give Nate much ability to aim, but Peggy was a sizable target at close range, so when he had a bead, he fired.

The bullet hit her in one meaty thigh and she screeched in pain. As she collapsed, she fired the shotgun.

With Granger on top of him as a human shield, Nate was spared the blast.

Granger moaned in agony then went limp.

Amazed he hadn't been hit, Nate shoved Granger off him while keeping his pistol trained on Peggy, who was laying on the floor flat on her back. She had dropped the shotgun.

Nate stood and adjusted his jacket which had been wrenched in every direction. He glanced at Granger. The skinny man's eyes stared at the wall, unblinking, copious amounts of blood pooling over the kitchen tiles beneath him.

Nate loomed over Peggy, who was mewling in pain. He pointed the pistol at her head.

"You know there's a word that describes the kind of day I've been having," he said, gasping heavily. "You know what word I'm talking about, Peggy?"

The woman was blubbering, shaking her head. "I don't... I don't..." she said.

"Cathartic," Nate said, and fired.

CHAPTER TWELVE

"Stay with me, buddy," Wyatt said, huffing and puffy. "We're almost there."

Truth was, he didn't know if they were or not. He'd carried Ethan over four blocks and there was still no sign of the clinic on either side of the street. Where was the damned place?

Ethan groaned, which Wyatt took as a good sign despite the circumstances. For the last block or so, he'd almost let himself be convinced his friend had died on his shoulder.

"Don't you worry," Wyatt said, skirting a semi-trailer which had run up onto the sidewalk. "You'll be in fine complaining form in no time."

People were everywhere, clogging the sidewalks or sitting in or around their vehicles. Barely anyone gave Wyatt and his burden a second glance.

No one wants to get involved, Wyatt thought. But could he blame them? He must have looked like a madman carrying around a dead body.

Finally, he came up to the edge of a long strip-mall. Glancing at the main signage next to the road he saw the words he'd been praying for: Elmdale Clinic.

"Oh, thank God," Wyatt said, and walked off the sidewalk to enter the strip-mall's parking lot. Cars were parked everywhere, dead vehicles blocking the lane-ways.

"Almost there," Wyatt said, over and over. "Almost there."

With his focus on the signs lining the storefronts, he didn't notice the slight dip a water drain created in the pavement. He stepped on the drain's angled edge and slipped.

With a cry of pain, he fell over. He twisted his body in a desperate attempt to shield Ethan from the fall. Wyatt hit the pavement hard with Ethan on top of him.

"Oh, shit!" Wyatt said. His left ankle exploded with pain which shot up his leg.

Ethan rolled off of Wyatt and flopped to the pavement. He was unconscious, eyes closed. Blood saturated his clothes all around the wound.

Wyatt grasped at his ankle, tears welling in his eyes. "This can't be happening. Not now!" He sat up and looked around for help. His view was blocked by cars and what few people he could see kept their distance or simply looked away.

"I need some help here!" Wyatt called out to anyone who would listen. No one came forward.

He leaned over Ethan and slapped his face harder than he'd done before. "Stay with me, buddy. We're here. We're at the clinic, just stay awake, okay?"

Ethan was unresponsive.

Wyatt checked the store front signs and saw a large one a few doors down. Elmdale Clinic.

He tried to get up, but the pain in his ankle kept him from standing. "God damnit!" Again, he looked around for help.

"Well, if it ain't Dopey and Sneezy," a familiar voice said from behind. Wyatt turned in alarm.

Casket stood in the middle of the lane, a wide grin on his face. Beside him was Scarface, pressing a rolled up sock against his bloody nose.

Both Feral Kids glared down at Wyatt and Ethan.

"Funny meeting you here, huh?" Casket said. "Looks like we had the same idea coming to the clinic. Thanks to your dumb ass, my boy here needs to get his nose looked at."

Scarface stepped forward and kicked Wyatt hard in the back. Wyatt tried to block it, but caught most of the blow.

Casket pulled Scarface back. "Now, now," he said looking around at the people who gawked at them. "No need to make a spectacle of ourselves."

"Bastard broke my nose!" Scarface said, his eyes were like daggers.

Wyatt said, "I'll break more than that if you don't leave us alone." It sounded feeble even to his ears, laying on the ground with a messed up ankle.

Casket leaned over. "Think anyone here gives a shit about you? Huh? If I slice off your skin right here and now, I bet no one will do anything but watch." He reached around his back and Wyatt realized it was for the Bowie-knife under his shirt.

"What in the hell is going on here?" a deep voice boomed.

A large security guard appeared from between some cars. He was massive in size, like one of those mutant wrestlers you see on television.

The guard looked from Wyatt and Ethan to the Feral Kids. "There won't be any fighting in my parking lot!"

Casket looked like he was going to charge the guard when he noticed the pistol holstered at the other man's hip. The Feral Kid took a step back.

"We don't want any problems, mister," Casket said. He gestured at Wyatt. "We were just looking to help these sad, pathetic bums. I think they're having issues."

Wyatt scowled at Casket, then turned to the guard. "Can you help me out? My friend here has been stabbed. I need to get him to the clinic."

The guard eyed Ethan, then removed some plastic gloves from a pocket to put them on. "He does look bad." He glanced to Casket and Scarface. "I got this. You two go about your business." His tone left no room for argument.

Casket and Scarface walked away toward the clinic, both grinning. From behind the guard's back, Scarface made a cutting motion across his throat with a finger. Wyatt tried to ignore him.

The guard hunched down. "Let's see if we can get him up." He reached under Ethan's arms and hoisted the man up like he was doll. To Wyatt, the guard asked, "How are you doing? You okay?"

Wyatt pushed himself up to stand, leaning against a car. "Yeah, my ankle is screwed up, but I'll be fine." He nodded to Ethan. "It's him I'm more worried about."

"Well, let's get him into the clinic. But I gotta warn you, shit's crazy in there." He walked backwards dragging Ethan.

Wyatt quickly picked up Ethan's legs and limped along behind the massive guard as they navigated their way through the parking lot.

The Elmdale Clinic's main entrance was crowded with people. Its double doors were propped open and Wyatt could see more folks inside. Amazingly, several roll away beds had been moved outside onto the sidewalk, occupied with patients.

Wyatt blinked in confusion at the sight of this. The guard noticed and said, "No power, so no lights of any kind. Even the backup system didn't so much as flicker on. So we had to move some people outside who's rooms didn't have windows. Thank God no major surgeries were going on."

As they passed through the doors and into the foyer it grew noticeably darker. All the shades on the large front windows had been pulled up, but what light they provided did little to lift the gloom further in the building.

Dozens of people were here. With all the chairs taken most sat along the walls or huddled in groups.

Medical staff ran about in a frenzy of activity bordering on full out panic.

"Hey, let's put your friend over here," the guard said indicating a section of wall. "Make room, please!" he barked at a couple of teenagers who leapt out of the way.

Wyatt helped ease Ethan down into a sitting position against the wall. "Shouldn't we take him in to see a doctor?"

The guard pointed over at a man in a white lab coat, hunched over a patient on a bed in the middle of the hallway. Nurses were assisting him, but their eyes were frantic. "That's the doctor. He was the only one here when the power went out. Now everyone needs him."

Wyatt was incredulous. The doctor was performing some kind of surgery right there out in the open.

"No lights in the operating room," the guard said. "And neither are there windows. So, we gotta make do."

Wyatt looked to Ethan with grave concern. "But my friend..."

The guard held up a hand. "I'll see what I can do. Everyone is now on triage, but I can't promise you anything.

"Triage..." Wyatt said. Is that what this has come down to?

"Yeah," the guard said, misinterpreting Wyatt. "Means the worst goes first." He looked at Ethan. "And he's one of them, that's for certain."

Suddenly, an argument broke out in front of the main entrance. People were yelling and shouting.

Without another word, the guard stood and rushed outside.

Wyatt looked to Ethan. "Hang in there, buddy. We made it. Just gotta wait for the doctor. He's coming to see you next. Don't you worry."

Ethan didn't respond.

He can't die, Wyatt thought. Ethan was all he had in the world when it came right down to it. Ethan was the only one who kept him in check. And without him around, Wyatt didn't even know what he would do with himself.

He felt somebody staring at him from across the waiting room.

Casket and Scarface stood next to the main reception desk. Both of them were glaring at Wyatt. Casket started blowing kissing at him and flicking his tongue out provocatively.

Wyatt knew right then and there that things were about to get a whole lot worse. He reached into his pocket and slipped on the brass knuckles.

Then rage exploded in his chest.

CHAPTER THIRTEEN

Nate

Nate arrived at Unger's bar, The Spectacular, roughly an hour or two before sundown. Without any ability to tell the time, he guessed it was five o'clock.

Along the way from Granger's, he passed no less than eight burning buildings. None had any firefighters attending to them and crowds gathered around to watch, helpless.

He'd seen even more carnage on the streets then was imaginable. This thing was city-wide, without a doubt. Not one car or motorbike or anything motorized moved. Nothing. Only people on bicycles like himself.

And the crowds outside got bigger and denser. It seemed like everyone was outside now. They sensed that something greater than a blackout had occurred. Something so significant that their lives might be changed. Everyone waited for the lights to come on, so the long agonizing process of untangling the Gordian-knot of a traffic jam could begin. But the lights didn't come back on and Nate was beginning to think they might never.

Which suited him just fine.

He rode his mountain bike across Spectacular's parking lot, which was empty except for a blue truck and a black Mercedes. The Mercedes was Unger's and Morse drove the truck.

Good, they were both here.

The front double doors were propped open with barstools. Two large men sat in either one, Wilson and Earl; Spectacular's bouncers, and Unger's goons.

Nate had hoped they wouldn't be here since their shift didn't start until the lunch hour, well after all cars in the cities had died. Yet, here they were.

The men eyed him as he rode up. "Gentlemen," Nate said with an affable smile. "Thought you guys would have the night off, all considering."

"Considering what?" Wilson growled. He was the nice one.

Nate leaned his bike up against a concrete barrier post. "Considering there isn't any electricity. Can't run a bar without it."

Wilson sniffed. "Fuck the electricity company. They're pulling a con, I say."

"Electrical company," Earl corrected.

"What?" said Wilson.

"It's called the electrical company," Earl said. Only Earl could correct Wilson, which was an ongoing thing for him. Earl held a lighter in his hand and flicked it on and off.

"Whatever," Wilson said. "Still a con. Now they can ask for anything they want to turn this shit back on."

Nate hated to interrupt such a fascinating conversation, but asked, "So, how did you guys get here? Bike?"

Both men turned to fix Nate with dour expressions.

"What do you care?" Wilson asked.

"Just curious," Nate said. They had their jackets off and were wearing shoulder holsters. Unger must have thought someone might take a run at him with all that was happening. He wasn't incorrect.

"We flew, alright?" Earl said. "You and your fucking questions."

Nate raised his hands, "Okay, fine. So much for small talk. Is Unger in?"

Wilson laughed. "Course Unger is in," Wilson said. "It's his bar. Why wouldn't he be in?"

I should have shot these guys as I rode up, Nate thought, exasperated. But he didn't really want to. As shitty an attitude these guys had, they were good muscle. And muscle would be very valuable in the days ahead.

Earl said, "The question isn't whether Unger is in, but whether Unger wants anything to do with you right now."

"I gotta report in," Nate said.

"Report what in?" Earl asked.

"The job I was on."

"What about it?"

Nate felt his temper rising. He couldn't flip off on these two. They may be huge, but their size was deceptive. He'd seen them draw their pistols before and they were both damned quick.

"Unger wants me to report in," Nate said through gritted teeth. "That's all I can say about it. You know how it is."

"No, how is it?" Wilson said, enjoying his little power trip.

Earl waved a hand at Nate. "Unger said nothing about you reporting in today. So it ain't gonna happen. Ride your bike home, Nate. If we want ya, we'll call."

Wilson burst into laughter. "Call! Ha! That's rich! No phones, Earl!"

Earl rolled his eyes. "Yeah, I know that, ya idiot."

Wilson chuckled and shook his head. "Call! Heheh."

Nate had had enough of this little show. He may need muscle in the future, but it didn't have to be these two assholes. He tensed up.

"Davenport! Get your ass in here!" came a booming shout from the dark bowels of the bar.

Wilson and Earl sat straighter on their stools.

Earl nodded toward the door. "Boss wants ya," he said, serious. His eyes gave Nate's long coat a once over.

Nate entered the bar which was nearly pitch black. A column of fading sun from the doorway created a corridor of light which sliced across the huge room, revealing tables and chairs, all empty. At the other end, the door to Unger's office could be seen with more light spilling into it from another source.

He crossed the bar, mindful of Earl's gaze on his back.

At the office door, he paused. The small room was dominated by a huge oak desk with a high-back, leather chair. The walls were covered in old photos of Unger posing with strippers and political figures which Nate found amusing. They both danced for money, but in different ways.

Boxing trophies crowded for space atop a filing cabinet. Unger had been a golden-gloves or something like it back in his younger days.

An ashtray on the desk caught Nate's attention. Ash and cigar stubs formed a small mountain range on it. It was shaped like a seashell just like the one Granger had.

Guess idiots do all shop at the same stores, he thought with a wry grin.

Where was Unger?

A prickling against his neck made him turn in alarm.

Earl stood there, watching him with a crooked smile.

Panic rose in Nate's chest and he was about to reach into his jacket when the other man pointed a finger.

"He's out back," Earl said, indicating a short hallway that led outside. The back door was open, revealing a parking lot. Nate could see someone's legs sitting on a chair outside.

Nate nodded at Earl and headed to the back door, mindful of the other man following.

Outside, Nate found Unger sitting in a plush chair dragged out from his office.

If there was one way to best describe Unger's appearance, it would be to take a grizzly bear and shave off all its fur. Kick it in the balls, to give it a perpetual expression of anger, then stick a cigar in its mouth.

The furless grizzly looked up at Nate and talked around his cigar. "Davenport. The fuck? Sit down," Unger said, pointing at another chair which held the door open.

Nate did as he was told. Earl took up a position in the doorway and leaned against the frame.

"Getting some fresh air, boss?" Nate asked. He didn't like how his jacket moved as he sat down, but it was long enough to still cover him almost to his knees.

Unger peered around the back parking lot. There was nothing here but bare concrete and a high fence. A column of black smoke rose up in the distance. Another fire.

"Yeah, well, there's no God-damned electricity," Unger said "Hasn't been all day. Can't see shit. Here, look at this." On the ground beside him were a half dozen flashlights. He scooped one up with a large knuckled hand and flicked its switch. Nothing happened. "They're all like that." He tossed the flashlight to the ground where it clattered across the concrete.

"Phones are dead, too," Nate said.

Unger nodded, a rare gesture from him considering he never agreed with anyone on anything. "All the damn phones are dead. All the cells, even the God-damned landline at the front."

Nate glanced between Earl and Unger. "So you haven't got word?" He let the question hang there like the smoke which curled from Unger's cigar.

The boss raised an eyebrow. "Word about what?"

Nate gave it a second. The man didn't take the bait. "That this thing is city wide. The whole place."

"Figured as much," Unger said. He looked to Earl. "Didn't I say that before?"

Earl grunted in agreement.

Unger's gaze fixed on Nate for several long moments, then said. "So, that thing."

"That thing is in the bag," Nate said.

"Done, eh?"

"Done and over."

"No problems?"

This last question almost tripped Nate up. *No problems, other than I had to shoot a cop who's a known enemy of your crew. Other than that, no problems.*

Nate shook his head. "None at all."

Unger listened with interest. He took a long drag from his cigar then exhaled it toward Nate.

Earl shifted, and no longer leaned against the door frame. He looked bored.

"Is that so?" Unger asked. "No problems, eh?"

Nate blinked. *What was this? He's giving me the third degree. Does he know about the path of carnage* Nate had been reaping across the city? *How?*

"Yeah," Nate said. He sat up a little, making it look like he was getting comfortable.

Unger stared at him through a veil of smoke. "Then why are you here, Nate?"

Alarm bells went off in Nate's head. *What the hell?* He found himself tensing, but made an effort not to show it. "I couldn't call it in like usual," Nate offered. "Figured I'd let you know face-to-face before I took my out." *That sounded plausible enough.*

Unger's gaze didn't flinch from Nate's. "Bit of a risk coming here, now, ain't it?"

The alarm bells had become a three alarm fire in Nate's head. He said, "Not really. Cops are busy right now. Can't even drive so I figured a visit was safe." His hands started to sweat.

A sudden loud noise made Nate blink away from Unger in confusion. Like metal being dragged across the concrete.

Unger frowned and turned to look behind him.

From the growing gloom a man emerged dragging a large metal barrel. He stopped in front of Unger and Nate and stood the barrel up between them.

Nate's apprehension vanished. Replaced by white hot anger.

It was Morse.

"Finally got it here," Morse said to Unger, panting heavily. "Had to drag it two blocks."

"No one gives a shit," Unger said. The big man hoisted himself up out of the chair and stood over the barrel, peering inside.

Nate took the opportunity to stand, too, giving him more freedom of movement.

Unger spat thickly into the empty barrel. "Well, fill it full of shit. It's gonna get dark in a minute."

Morse nodded and gave Nate a hateful glance, then went inside.

Nat stood next to the barrel, positioning it so it was between him and the other men. "What's this for? Bonfire?"

"Kinda," Unger said. His demeanor was hard to read. Was he hostile or had Nate misread their conversation? "Gonna have a barbecue. Cook up some of the steaks in the freezer before they go bad." He kicked at the barrel. "Do it cave man style, over a real fire."

Morse reappeared with a stack of newspapers under one arm and pieces of an old wooden chair under the other. He dropped them into the barrel and took the lighter from Earl.

Unger stared at Nate while Morse worked. "Was there something more you wanted to tell me, Nate?"

Morse lit the newspapers, and the fire sputtered to life. He looked from Unger to Nate with growing apprehension.

Might as well pull this band-aid off, myself, Nate thought.

"I killed a cop today," Nate said with a smile.

Unger did a double take. "What?"

"Yup," Nate said. "You know her, too. Victoria Lang. Or maybe that's *knew* her, past tense."

The furless grizzly glared at him over the crackling fire. "You're shitting me."

"Nope. I don't shit. Not about killing cops."

Morse stared at Nate in amazement and stepped back from the barrel. Behind him, Earl no longer looked bored, eyes fixed on Nate.

Nate continued into the silence. "Then I killed Jonas Anderson. Tossed him through a window."

Unger's cigar threatened to drop from his open mouth, stunned.

"After that, I paid a visit to a special friend of yours. Granger." He glared at his boss. "Figured it was the least I could do."

"You fuck," Unger said, recovering from these revelations. "You fucking fuck!"

"Aren't you gonna ask why?" Nate said.

Earl went for his pistol, but Nate was quicker. From beneath his long jacket he unslung a sawed-off shotgun from under his arm. The chamber was already loaded.

The blast sent Earl flying back through the open door and sprawling onto the floor.

The cigar dropped from Unger's mouth as he looked at his dead henchman.

Nate racked another round into the sawed-off's chamber and leveled it at Unger. "Go on, ask me why."

Unger glared at Nate with rage, but refused to do what he was told. No one told him what to do.

"Why?" asked Morse with a meek voice.

"Cause you had Chris killed. Raped and killed. Didn't you?" Nate asked.

Unger clenched his fists at his sides, wanting to get close to Nate. Become that boxer of old, again.

Since he didn't answer, Nate said, "I'll tell you why. Because-."

Wilson flew through the back door, pistol firing.

Nate felt a bullet hit him in the chest on his left pectoral. It was like getting kicked by a mule. But he stood firm and shot at Wilson, who was firing as quick as he could pull the trigger.

Nate's shot hit the henchman right in the face, spraying blood and brains everywhere. Wilson flopped to the ground.

Unger made a move toward Nate, but Nate pointed the sawed-off at him as he racked a new round, stopping the big man in his tracks.

"You gonna answer me?" Nate said, gasping for breath. His chest blossomed with incredible pain. Part of his left arm had gone completely numb, but he still had a firm grip on his weapon.

Morse had stood rooted to the spot during the entire exchange, hands in the air, terrified. When Unger refused to speak, he said, "He was gonna talk."

"Bullshit!" Nate said. "He would never have talked." The thought of Chris, his old friend, as a rat was too impossible to consider.

"Maybe," Unger finally said. "Maybe not. He was in for murder. Twenty years. Who knows what he would have said to get that reduced. He knew a lot of shit."

Nate could barely contain his rage. "So you had him killed. Didn't you? On the chance a loyal soldier might squeal?"

Unger shrugged. "It's how it's done. Couldn't take the risk." He said this in a matter-of-fact way, like he was describing how to properly smoke a cigar.

"Why Caleb? He wasn't a threat to you."

Unger's eyes flashed with anger. "Oh, no? Brother of the guy I had offed? It was only a matter of time before he figured it out or someone told him. Had to be done."

"Had to be done, huh?" Nate said and shot Unger in the knee.

The big man collapsed to the pavement shrieking in pain.

"Like that?"

Unger clasped at his ruined knee, blood gushing over the ground. He was surrounded by a half dozen cigar butts, the ones he'd smoked that day. "Fuck you, Nate! I should never have taken you on. Shoulda slit your throat myself!"

"Yeah," Nate said. "You really shoulda, Unger." He shot his boss in the face.

"Oh, God!" Morse said, looking down at Unger. His hands were still in the air. "You're crazy! Why did you do this? This isn't how shit gets done!"

Nate racked another round and pulled open his shirt to reveal a flat metal slug nestled in his bullet proof vest. "Why did I do this? That's a good question, Morse."

His gaze went over the darkening horizon. Two more columns of smoke had joined the first. Far in the distance, he heard rapid gunplay. Someone else must have been settling scores, too.

There is opportunity in chaos.

"I'll tell you why. Because I believe this is the start of a new era." He leveled the shotgun at Morse and smiled. "And I'm going to be the one leading the way."

Then he fired.

CHAPTER FOURTEEN

Wyatt

Brass knuckles in hand, and an angry fire blazing in his chest, Wyatt stood up. His ankle hurt like a son of a bitch, but he didn't care. All he wanted right then was to make Casket hurt. And hurt bad.

Across the waiting room, both Casket and Scarface noticed his change in demeanor. Casket slowly reached around his back and kept his hand there. He made a motion at Wyatt with his free hand. Come on.

But before Wyatt could move, the doctor suddenly appeared in front of him, blocking his view of the Feral Kids.

"This is your friend who was stabbed, yes?" the doctor said, looking down at Ethan.

Wyatt blinked in surprise, trying to push aside his anger. "Yeah, he's been cut bad. Been bleeding out for a while now." Was he babbling? After so long, it felt like a dream an actual doctor was right here, looking to help.

The doctor knelt down next to Ethan. He put his fingers against Ethan's neck. "How long ago was it?"

Casket was still motioning at Wyatt, come on. "What? Oh, uh, this morning around eight-thirty, I think."

The doctor looked up at Wyatt in alarm. "He's been bleeding this entire time?"

"Yeah, I couldn't get him to the hospital, you know. No ambulances or phones." Was the doctor mad at him?

The doctor motioned for some orderlies to bring over a gurney. Gently, they eased Ethan onto it. Ethan was completely limp. Wyatt couldn't tell if he was breathing anymore.

The doctor used a stethoscope on Ethan's chest. Then he quickly barked an order at a nurse and she placed a hand-pumped rebreather over Ethan's mouth and started squeezing. The doctor stood over Ethan

91

and placed his hands over the middle of his chest and pushed down, hard. CPR.

Oh, God! Wyatt thought staring at what was happening in total disbelief. He can't die! Not now! Not after I brought him all this way!

The doctor pressed down over and over on Ethan's chest so hard that Wyatt feared he'd break some ribs.

The surrounding people went quiet, watching.

A movement tore Wyatt's eyes away from his dying friend. Casket and Scarface were pointing at Ethan and pantomiming laughter, enjoying the scene.

Wyatt stood frozen. He looked to Ethan's face, covered by the rebreather. The doctor worked frantically.

He didn't know how long it was, but after a while Wyatt realized the doctor had stopped. The doctor shook his head, reached to Ethan's face at his vacant open eyes and gently closed them.

No, no, no, this can't be happening, Wyatt thought. A rush of emotion surged through his body. This can't be happening! He got him here to the clinic! He can't die now!

The doctor turned to Wyatt with a somber expression. Over his shoulder, Casket and Scarface were guffawing silently, slapping each other on the back.

"I'm sorry," the doctor said. "Your friend has passed away. If he'd had gotten here sooner, or if we had electricity, we might have-." But the doctor didn't get to finish before Wyatt suddenly lunged forward.

Wyatt knocked the doctor aside, and charged at Casket.

Casket, expecting some sort of reaction, suddenly whipped out his large knife.

People screamed.

In an instant, Wyatt crossed the distance between them and collided with Casket. Casket tried to stab at Wyatt, but the old hobo caught his arm with a vice-like grip.

Wyatt's momentum pushed them back against a wall where people leapt out of the way. As they hit the wall, Casket head-butted Wyatt in the cheek causing him to see stars, but the hobo kept on fighting. He smashed the Feral Kid in the face with the knuckles.

Casket suddenly collapsed to his knees, the knife wielding hand going limp.

Scarface hit at Wyatt's back like it was a punching bag. Wyatt grunted with each hit. Calmly, he reached down and took the knife from Casket's hand. Then he slashed backward with it and a red line appeared across Scarface's throat.

Wide-eyed, Scarface stumbled back, clutching at his neck where blood geysered from the wound. With shock, he locked eyes with Wyatt then tumbled to the ground, gasping.

Wyatt spun around to face Casket. "This is for Ethan, you shit." He jabbed the large knife straight into Casket's face, right to its hilt.

Casket fell to the ground, dead.

Wyatt stood, gasping, a strange calm washing over him.

The massive guard ran in from outside and took in the scene. Quickly, he unholstered his pistol and pointed it at Wyatt with both hands. "Drop the knife!"

Wyatt looked about in a daze; Casket dead at his feet, Scarface convulsing on the ground in a widening pool of blood.

"Drop the knife, now!"

"You better do as he says," Wyatt heard someone say. He looked over at Ethan on the gurney.

Ethan was looking at him, alive as ever.

"Ethan?" Wyatt said, confused. "But you're dead! I saw you die!"

Ethan shrugged. "Yeah, well shit happens. Least I died wearing nice shoes. Better than most can say." No one seemed to notice that he was speaking, all eyes on Wyatt. "But what good would all of this have been for if you joined me now?"

Wyatt blinked in confusion, then looked at the pistol pointed at him. He willed it to shoot.

"Don't do that," admonished Ethan's corpse. "Your time isn't now. You know that. There is work to do."

Wyatt's mind reeled. This was all too familiar, but he couldn't remember where, or from when.

"Drop the knife! I won't say it again!" yelled the guard, a look of pleading was in his eyes. He didn't want to do it, but he would if that's what Wyatt wanted.

Is that what I want? he thought to himself. He looked to Ethan, again, for guidance.

Ethan's body lay still on the gurney, eyes closed.

There is still work to do.

Wyatt dropped the knife, and it clattered to the floor. He placed his hands behind his head.

He had the sense he was being handcuffed, but it didn't fully register. Instead, he gazed at the bloody carnage at his feet. A realization dawning on him.

Oh, no, he thought. I've done it again.

CHAPTER FIFTEEN

Nate

Sitting amongst the corpses, Nate watched the city burn.

The night sky was flush with stars, bright and eager to be seen. Nate could not remember the last time he'd seen the stars like this. Childhood?

There was a time when his asshole father took him and his mother on a camping trip. Like everything else about his father, it was a joke. The man drunk himself into oblivion, pissing into the camp fire. When his mom complained, his father started to beat her. Despite being only eight or nine, Nate tried to defend her and was beaten in turn.

The stars were beautiful back then, too.

Ah, memories.

But now that he thought about it, these stars were unusually bright. Like thousands of little spotlights trying to illuminate the chaos below.

Over the fence, across the bar's back parking lot, fires burned in the distance. Nate couldn't see them directly, but their hot glow pushed against the night like little suns trying to break up out of the horizon.

Nate had his own fire, thanks to Morse the screw-up. The flames within the barrel flickered and crackled. When it started to die down, Nate went into Unger's office and found more things to burn. Nate chose a bunch of Unger's photos and a mound of bills and papers from the desk.

He dumped them in and the fire blazed.

"Won't be needing those anymore, eh, boss?" Nate said to Unger's cooling corpse.

Not getting an answer, Nate went and sat back down in one of the comfy chairs, shotgun across his lap.

He listened to the sound of the fire. Somewhere, far off, popping indicated a rifle being used. He'd heard more throughout the night as he sat there and watched the city die. Old scores needed to be settled and what better time to do it?

Nate had many of his own to get to. The list was long with only a few names being of distinguishing merit. But they were all shit that needed to be shoveled.

He patted the shotgun. This was his shovel.

A squishy noise emanated from Morse, causing Nate to raise his rifle. When he recognized it as a body expelling gas, he laughed.

"Full of shit both in life and in death," Nate said. "Not surprised."

Morse responded with more death farts.

Nate fished a beer out of a small cooler next to the chair and examined the label in the fire light. God damned german import. Unger always had bad taste in drink. Nate shrugged, twisted off the cap and took a swig.

He grimaced. Bitter and heavy, just like Unger and his family.

Unger's family.

In a normal situation, Nate would be running for his life right now, having gunned downed the organization's up and comer. He didn't have permission to take Unger out, nor would he have ever sought it. That would have been a death sentence, being just a piddly gun-for-hire. A contract would be put on his head and the countdown would begin. Nate was certain he could have given any would-be bounty hunters a run for their money.

But this wasn't a normal situation. He doubted things would ever be normal again.

It made him smile.

A sudden scream from his left made him drop the beer bottle with a smash and stand up, shotgun at the ready. It had come from the little apartment building located next door to the Spectacular. There were a couple of windows which had small pulses of glowing candles. One of them was brighter than the rest and growing brighter. Frantic shadow puppets danced around inside, trying to put out the errant flames.

Nate laughed and dragged the chair over so he could see better. He grabbed another bitter beer and sat down to enjoy the show. This little sun was closer than the rest, eager to be born.

For nearly twenty minutes, he watched as the fire went out of control and consumed the little apartment. Soon its flames licked out from the open balcony window, the curtains coiling into hot ash.

As he watched, he thought about what his next move would be. Killing Unger was an automatic death sentence, but only if other's found out about it. Or if he got to them first.

And with this strange day drawing to an end, Nate felt certain Unger's death would rank fairly low on priorities to those who might care. The world was being reborn, like these little suns.

No alarms sounded from the apartment building. The little batteries in the smoke detectors had been nixed along with everything else.

Maybe it was what the aliens intended. Kill the batteries. Kill the electricity. Let humanity kill itself.

Nate took another swig and watched the apartment fire spread across the floors. Who was he to try and understand what this event was meant to accomplish? To the aliens, he was nothing more than another human they hoped would die in an apartment fire.

But Nate felt he was more than that and would prove it. If anything, he was an opportunist and had shown he could grab an opportunity by the hair and make it his bitch.

"Hello?" a voice called out.

Nate blinked out of his thoughts. It had come from inside the bar. Quietly, he placed the beer on the ground and went over to the open back door, shotgun in both hands. He peered inside.

Other than the orange flickering light from the barrel fire, he couldn't make out anything past Unger's office at the end of the little hall.

"Hello?" the voice said, again. It was a man. Sounded like he was in the main room of the bar.

Nate entered and walked down the hall, shotgun pointed forward ready to spit out death. When he reached the office, he noticed another light through the office door, this one coming from within the bar itself. Someone with a light source?

With a glance behind him, Nate moved to the office door and peeked around its frame.

A man was standing in the middle of the bar, short and fat. A lantern sat on a table next to him, its inner flame bright and strong.

A quick look told Nate the man was not carrying any weapons in his hands, but he needed to be cautious.

Certain there was no one else present, Nate stepped through the door.

The fat man gave a quivering start when he noticed Nate. "Oh, damn," he said. "You scared me. I didn't think anyone was around."

"I'm scary," Nate said as he approached. "And I'm around." He kept two tables between them, the shotgun pointed at the other man. "Who are you?"

The man glanced at the shotgun with wide eyes and slowly raised his empty hands. "Hey, I'm just here to make a delivery. No need to get all worried about it."

"I'm not worried. Who are you?"

"Martin," the fat man said. Wide spots of sweat stained his shirt. Nate could see the man was shaking.

"Hello, Martin, I'm Nate."

When Nate didn't say anymore, Martin said, "Hello, Nate." He swallowed hard.

"What are you delivering today? Better not be anymore of that crappy german beer because that would put me in a really foul mood."

Martin shook his head. "No, no crappy german beer."

Fear kept the man from speaking. "Then what?" Nate said.

"Prawns."

Nate burst into laughter. When he settled down, he shook a finger at Martin, shotgun still held steady. "Ah, Marty, I did not expect you to say that. Beer, sure. But prawns?"

Martin shrugged. "Unger likes them, even though they don't sell very well, here."

"Yeah, who comes to a bar to eat prawns trucked in from an ocean which is miles and miles away."

"They're from Japan," Martin said, looking worried he might be speaking out of turn. "Unger likes those, especially."

Nate laughed, again, this time louder and longer. "Oh, that is funny, Marty." He looked around. "Where are these Japanese prawns? I know you didn't bring them in a truck."

Martin shook his head. "No, my truck died on the freeway this morning. Along with everyone else."

Nodding, Nate said, "Yeah, that was one hell of a morning, wasn't it?"

"It's been one hell of a day," Martin said, relaxing a little. He pointed a thumb toward the front doors. "Got 'em outside."

Nate nodded for Martin to start walking. "Well, show me these imported Japanese prawns."

When Martin picked up the lantern and turned, Nate nearly shot him, right then and there. This man was dead weight. And if he sees the bodies out the back, he'd be a witness to Nate's crime.

But he didn't shoot the prawn man, not yet. Something about him made Nate curious.

Instead of blasting a hole in the fat man's back, he followed him out the front doors, which were still propped open by the stools vacated by Earl and Wilson.

"Here they are," Martin said.

A wheel-barrel sat near the edge of the walkway, stuffed with plastic bags marked with the stylised symbol of a big prawn.

Nate looked them over. "You hauled these here with that?"

"Yup," Martin said, wiping sweat from his forehead for emphasis. "When the truck went tits up, I hoofed it back to the warehouse and grabbed the wheel-barrel. Then came back to the truck and filled up as much as I could."

"There's more?"

"Yeah, but the refrigeration in the truck died with the rest of it, so I expect they've gone bad by now in this heat."

"How far did you come?"

"Third avenue. Took me eight hours to get here."

Nate was impressed, but frowned in confusion. "Then why bother bringing these all the way here if they were just going to go bad along the way?"

Martin shrugged. "I iced them up real good, but that melted away after the first two hours." His voice trailed off as if he didn't want to say anymore.

Then Nate understood. "You wanted Unger to know you tried."

"Yeah," Martin said, a little sheepishly. "If I didn't do anything, or didn't show I made an effort to get him some of his prawns here, there'd be hell to pay."

Nate watched the fat man as he spoke. He recognized that look. Defeat. Fear. Here was an employee of Unger's who knew the boss was unforgiving, let alone even fair, when it came to mistakes. Even ones that were completely out of his control.

Nate lowered his shotgun. "Well, Unger won't be needing these prawns at all."

Martin looked confused. "He won't?" He glanced into the bar. "Isn't he here? He's always here."

"Oh, he's here. Maybe you can go explain to him what happened."

"O-okay," Martin said with some hesitation. He led them both through the bar, again, with his lantern.

Curious, Nate asked, "Where did you get that lantern?"

"Had it in the warehouse," Martin said as they navigated around empty tables. The bar looked ghostly in the lantern's flickering light. "Always wanted to use it and now I got the chance."

Nate smiled. "I think we'll be using it quite a bit from now on." In all honesty, he liked what he saw in this Martin guy. A go-getter willing to do what it took to impress his boss.

A potential lackey.

They entered the office and Nate pointed the shotgun at the back hallway. "Out there," he said.

Martin walked outside then stopped when he noticed all the bodies.

Nate kept his shotgun low, but held it so he could bring it up in a flash.

The fat man scanned over the carnage with wide eyes. His gaze settled on Unger's corpse. He blinked and walked over to it.

"He's dead," Martin said.

"That would be his current state, yes," Nate said. The apartment next door was in full bloom, its fire out of control. But, neither he, nor Martin, bothered to look.

Martin said, "Did you kill him?"

Nate pondered his answer, then simply said, "Yup."

Anger rippled across the little man's face. "Bastard!" Martin reached for the front of his pants.

Surprised at this sudden change in demeanor, Nate raised his shotgun ready to add another body to the back lot's inventory.

But instead of pulling out a gun, Martin fumbled open his fly and pulled out his dick.

Stunned, Nate watched as Martin pissed on Unger's corpse.

"I was supposed to be the one that killed him," Martin said through gritted teeth.

Nate laughed loudly in genuine delight. What a sight to see as this little fat man emptied his bladder on the body of his old boss. "He pissed you off, too, huh?"

"Yeah," Martin said, angling the stream to spatter Unger's ruined face. "And now I get to piss off him."

Nate laughed some more. He liked this Martin guy and decided he wouldn't kill him after all.

No, he thought. I'll keep him for myself

CHAPTER SIXTEEN

"Murderer!"

The woman's scream snapped Wyatt out of his trance. He'd been staring down at his sneakers, watching the pool of blood flow around them.

The other people in the clinic were running for the door, pushing to get out.

To get away from him.

"Don't move," the security guard said from behind him. Wyatt felt his wrists being cinched together. Not handcuffs, he knew what those felt like. Plastic ties. Good.

"You've made a hell of a mess," the guard said as he grasped Wyatt's arm. His grip was like a vice, strong and unbreakable. "People come here to keep from dying, not the other way around."

Wyatt was struck by the odd comment. He'd just murdered two of the Feral Kids right here in the middle of the clinic's lobby in front of dozens of witnesses, and this guy was making jokes?

The bodies of Scarface and Casket lay contorted on the floor. Casket with a knife wound through his face, and Scarface with his throat slashed wide open like a crimson grin.

"They were laughing at Ethan," Wyatt mumbled.

"Shut up," said the guard.

After Wyatt killed the Feral Kids the doctor of the clinic had leapt into action, trying to save both of the them. But a quick assessment told the story. Neither Casket, nor Scarface, would be tormenting any more homeless again.

The doctor leaned over Casket's face, looking at the fatal wound. "God damnit," he said. He looked up at Wyatt with an expression of confusion. "Why did you do this?"

"It was their time," Wyatt said with a dismissive shrug. "The world is a better place now." His tone was casual, but he meant what he said. Killing them felt right, now that it was over and done with. The impulse had rushed through him, carrying him along like a twig on the shoulders of a mighty river. There was nothing he could have done to stop himself. It had to be.

The doctor shook his head then said to the guard, "Get him out of here!" He rubbed at his glasses and smeared blood along his nose.

"Where?" the guard asked. "Outside?"

The waiting area was now clear of people, most of whom stood clustered outside the front windows in the growing dark. Wyatt could hear their chattering, terrified and excited. Some stared at him with shock and horror.

A nurse stood cowering behind the reception desk, eyes locked on the two bodies.

The doctor waved at her. "Peggy! Go grab my keys in my office, quickly."

The nurse blinked in confusion and after casting a glance at Wyatt, hurried off down the dark hallway.

"You'll put him in my truck for now until the police come," the doctor said, moving over to look at the crimson smile across Scarface's throat.

"Maybe we should lock him in a room," the guard said. "It would make more sense." Despite the chaos Wyatt had just caused, the guard wasn't rattled. Like a double homicide was something he dealt with on a regular basis. Wyatt couldn't decide if that was a character trait he liked or should be suspicious of.

The doctor stood. "All the rooms are occupied." He pointed at Wyatt with a trembling finger. "And besides, I don't want him anywhere near our patients."

Wyatt felt disappointed. He would have thought the doctor could have been more calm in such a situation. Obviously, he'd never been a combat medic which, considering how things were shaping up outside, would be a good skill to have.

The nurse returned and handed the keys to the doctor.

"Do we have any candles?" the doctor asked her. He dropped the keys into the guard's huge hand.

"Candles? Uh, no. Not at all," she said, casting furtive glances in Wyatt's direction. She was pretty. Older, maybe in her mid-forties, but that didn't bother Wyatt. He liked women in uniform.

The doctor waved at the guard. "What is this maniac still doing here? Get him out and watch him!"

The guard pulled Wyatt around the bodies, their shoes leaving bloody impressions on the linoleum tiles. "Watch your step," the guard said as they passed Ethan's body on the gurney.

He let himself be guided to the front doors which were still propped open. As Wyatt and the guard moved outside, the crowd of people backed away, some gasping.

"Excuse us," the guard said, and escorted Wyatt over to a giant hatchback parked nearest the door.

Figures the doctor would have the best spot, Wyatt thought as the guard took him to the passenger side door and fumbled with the keys in his hand.

Wyatt looked over the darkening parking lot and out at the main street. Cars, trucks and buses were lined up in both direction, bumper to bumper and stock still. No one moved. Things had not changed much since Wyatt took Ethan into the clinic.

Now he knew it was all for the better.

"This is a good thing," Wyatt mumbled.

"What?" the guard said, finally unlocking the door and opening it. "What did you say?"

Wyatt offered the man a syrupy grin. "This is all a good thing that's happened. Trust me on that." He felt the conviction down in his bones.

"Uh-huh," the guard said, and shoved Wyatt up into the passenger seat. With his hands restrained behind his back, it made sitting uncomfortable.

"I'm not comfortable," Wyatt said. He felt sleepy, like a nap was needed now more than ever.

"Shut up, and don't cause any problems," the guard said. Confident Wyatt was secured, he fished a phone out of his uniform's front pocket.

Wyatt watched him with pity and shook his head. "No need for those anymore, friend. Today has changed that."

The guard thumbed the buttons on the phone which looked like a toy in his massive hand. The screen remained dark. No rings or beeps. "Damnit," the guard said.

Wyatt watched him for a few moments as he futilely tried to resurrect the little device. "Do you know what is going to happen?"

The guard looked up and arched a brow at Wyatt. "Yeah, I know what's going to happen."

"What?"

"I'm going to hand you over to the police, is what's going to happen. Then I'm going to submit an overtime sheet and demand a danger pay bonus."

"Danger pay?" Wyatt laughed. The term was odd to hear out loud. "That's not what I meant."

"Okay, what do you mean?" The guard looked frustrated. Wyatt felt for him, he was having a rough day. Something Wyatt could identify with.

"You're not going to hand me over to the police," Wyatt said.

The guard scoffed. "Oh, no? What am I going to do with you then?"

"You're going to let me go."

The guard laughed, a deep barking sound. "That's rich. You really expect that, huh? Murder two people in my clinic and just waltz away?"

"No, you're going to let me go because I have a job to do."

"And what's that? Kill more people?"

Wyatt shook his head, the approaching night felt like cotton against his senses. "I didn't kill people," he nodded toward the clinic and the bodies inside. "Those weren't people."

The expression on the guard's face said he thought Wyatt was nuts. "If those aren't people, then what are they?"

"A beginning," Wyatt said, smiling wide. He rested his head back against the seat.

The guard scoffed again. "Damn nut-job. Murderous, killing nut-job. But you still didn't answer my question."

"Which was?" Wyatt said through lidded eyes.

"Why would I let you go after what you just did?"

"Because I have a job to do, and not you, nor anyone else, can stop me from doing it."

"What job is that?"

Wyatt thought for a moment, then said, "I don't know. It's not clear to me, yet."

Some people at the front of the clinic starting yelling at each other. Then a man pushed a younger woman against a glass window, causing it to rattle.

"Hey!" the guard said. To Wyatt he said, "Stay put and don't be stupid." He slammed the door and went over to the brawling couple shouting for everyone to calm down.

Wyatt watched as the guard tried to maintain order. Even despite his size, things were getting out of hand. The people were agitated. Not just at what Wyatt had done, but the fact that this entire situation was confusing, and it wasn't getting any clearer.

He looked over each one, men and women, husbands and wives. They were all at the start of a great change. Sort of like himself, only Wyatt knew his change was for a greater purpose. What it was, he couldn't be sure, but he wasn't worried. He'd get a sign soon enough.

A strange sereneness passed over his body as he contemplated the possibilities of what his new job would be. Whatever it was, it would finally give him something more to strive for than simple survival. No more dumpsters, no more cans, no more bottles. No more being afraid.

Killing Casket and Scarface had dislodged something inside him. A jagged thing which had been stuck in his soul for so long he'd forgotten to even dream anymore. Now, he was in a dream.

"Penny for your thoughts?"

Wyatt turned to the voice. Ethan was sitting in the driver's seat, looking at him with a wide grin.

"You're dead," Wyatt said. "What's up with that?"

Ethan shrugged. "Can't say for sure. Only I know it has something to do with you, of all people. Damned if I can figure out why."

Wyatt looked Ethan over. His friend looked just as he was before Casket had sliced him up. Rough and ready for a day of dumpster diving. Was he an angel? He didn't look it. But he didn't smell bad anymore. In fact, Wyatt was certain Ethan smelled like peppermint.

"No," Wyatt said, sitting up. "You're dead. I saw you die. Then you talked to me from that gurney like nothing had happened. Now you're here in the doctor's truck like it was something I wanted."

Ethan looked around the truck's cab and placed his hands on the wide steering wheel. "This is the doctor's truck? Damn fine set of wheels, if you ask me. Guess he could afford it, being a doctor and all. Although I think he kind of sucks at his job, considering he couldn't save me." His face scrunched up in thought. "Do doctors have their pay cut when someone dies in their care?"

Wyatt shook his head, his eyes never leaving Ethan. He was here. Really here in the truck. Wyatt could feel his presence just as if someone alive would be. "Why are you here?"

"Enjoying this fine example of American automotive craftsmanship!"

"No," Wyatt said, shaking his head. "Why are you here for me? Are you a figment of my imagination? Am I suffering a trauma of some kind?"

Ethan's smile slipped a little as he matched his friend's stare. "I'm not a figment of anything. I'm your friend and always will be. Trust me on that. And as for suffering a trauma," he waved his hands at the darkness around them and the people clustered outside, "the entire universe is suffering a trauma on a massive scale. But it doesn't have to be that way. It doesn't have to be as painful as it might be, unless something happens to ease them through this great change."

Wyatt blinked in confusion. "Gibberish. Pure Gibberish. You're not Ethan. At least, not the Ethan I knew. You're something else."

"No, Wyatt," Ethan said. "I'm still me. Only now I've changed, just like everyone else out there is changing, only they don't know it, yet. But they will, they certainly will."

"Yeah?" Wyatt said, feeling his anger grow. "And how do I fit into all this? You said I had a job to do. What is it?"

Ethan matched Wyatt's gaze. "Because your job is to save them."

CHAPTER SEVENTEEN

Nate

"I think you've earned yourself a bitter beer," Nate said. He handed Martin a bottle from the cooler. "In case you wanted to reload for another round."

Martin twisted off the cap and took a sip, his hands trembling.

"Here," Nate said, pointing to one of the chairs. "Take a load off."

Martin dropped into it and sighed. He looked exhausted and Nate suspected it was from more than the day long hike pushing a wheel-barrel of prawns. It was his mind that was tired.

Nate sat in the other chair across from the little fat man. "Sorry I stole your thunder," he said.

"What do you mean?" Martin asked. His eyes were watery as if he might burst into tears.

"Killing Unger," Nate said. "I know a lot of people had it out for him, but I was the one who got to pop that cherry."

Martin waved a hand. "No, don't apologize. The bastard deserved it. The things he did to me..."

Not sure he was ready for a sob story, Nate said, "He did a lot of crappy things to a lot of people. That was pretty much his job, after all. But he got his comeuppance and there's no taking it back."

"I know. I just didn't expect him to be dead so soon. I thought there would be time for me to find a way to get to him."

"Like a poisoned prawn?"

Martin laughed. "Or maybe a poisoned import beer."

Nate spit out his beer and laughed. "Okay, that was good one."

Both men went quiet for a time. Nate, leaning back and looking at the stars, Martin, staring into the dying fire in the barrel.

Martin finally asked, "Did they attack you?" He motioned to the other bodies with his beer bottle.

"More or less. They tried to rescue their king and were slain for their efforts." He was impressed this guy wasn't rattled at the sight of so many dead.

Martin looked the bodies over. "You killed all of them yourself?"

Nate didn't have to answer. He just took another swig.

"Damn," Martin said. "That's impressive."

They both watched the apartment burn, like the fire was possessed with unfettered rage. If people had escaped, they didn't do it from this side of the building. The heat was intense, and the flames brightened the back lot as if it were day.

"So what happens now?" Martin asked.

Nate knew he wasn't talking about the burning apartment. "I dunno," he said with a shrug. "What do you want to happen?"

Martin shook his head. "I'm at a loss. I'd resigned myself to having to work for this asshole for the rest of my life, or until I found a way to kill him. Now none of that matters."

This was music to Nate's ears, yet he still wasn't sure about this guy, having just met him. So he asked, "What if we were to go try and help those people?"

Martin looked to the burning apartment. "Are you kidding? Why would we do that? If we go try to help, then their problems become our problems. And, I dunno about you, but I got my fill already."

Nate chuckled. Okay, he thought, this guy isn't a total fool.

The smoke from the apartment inferno drifted over to where they sat, ruining their little get together.

"Let's move this party inside," Nate said, standing. "Besides, these guys are starting to really smell."

Nate followed Martin into the bar where they sat at one of the tables close to the front doors. The smoke was barely noticeable in here. Even the occasional screams from the apartments were muffled.

Peaceful.

"Are you armed?" Nate asked.

"Only with a bad attitude," Martin said.

"You're going to need more than that from now on," Nate said. "As you know, the shit has hit the fan and things have changed."

"But this can't last too long, can it? The power will come back on tomorrow, or soon after. It has to."

Nate reveled at the sound of desperate confusion in Martin's voice. "I don't think so. I believe this is the end-game which has fallen upon us and we need to get prepared."

"I dunno. It's possible this could be fixed real soon."

"Yeah, but does your phone work?"

Martin fished out a little phone from his back pocket and tossed it on the table. "Dead. Like everyone else's I've run into. Yours?"

"Very dead. Just like the cars and smoke detectors and planes, everything is dead that isn't even hooked up to the power grid. I haven't seen one electronic device of any kind working since this morning. Have you?"

Martin shook his head. "No, not a spark of life from anything electrical. The roads are complete chaos. People hollering and screaming. Pandemonium."

Nate chuckled. "Pandemonium. Good word. I like that. Covers exactly what's going on. No power of any kind anywhere has led to complete pandemonium. So do you really believe that this can be fixed overnight?"

"No way."

"Right. This is the ultimate dick-punch. A dick-punch to society as a whole. Maybe even the world."

"That's a pretty big dick-punch."

"And I'm going to go out on a limb and suggest that, even if they somehow manage to reverse this colossal dick-punch, things will not return to the way people are used to."

Martin nodded. "Too much damage has been done."

"And many scores being settled. There is a purge occurring out there tonight, and will continue to happen for days and weeks if not longer. How can a civilized society recover from that? I mean, really?"

Martin thought on this for a few moments. Nate drank his beer and watched him.

Martin said, "I think you're right."

"About?"

"About getting prepared. We need to protect ourselves. Get supplies and stuff."

Nate nodded. "We can't just sit around and wait for the government to come in and save our asses, now can we?"

"Uh-uh."

"They're too busy saving their own butts right now, mark my words."

"Yeah."

"So I think the best thing we could do is just as you said, get supplies and stuff. And by stuff, I mean weapons."

"I have a pistol back at the warehouse which is also full of canned crap we could use."

Nate smiled. "I like that, Marty. A man after my own heart."

Martin's eyes lit up, and he stood. "Hey, don't those guys out there have guns?"

"Yeah," Nate said.

"Uh, want me to go get 'em?"

Nate shook his head. "No need, I stashed them already." It was the first thing he did after plugging Morse. Can't have any guns laying about that weren't in his control so he stuffed them under Unger's desk for the moment.

"Oh, okay," Martin said, and sat back down. He took a sip of his beer.

Nate wasn't quite ready to give this guy a weapon, but what choice did he have? Things were spiraling out of control, and having him armed would be helpful. Could he trust him?

After some thought, Nate reached into his jacket's deep pocket and pulled out his pistol. "Here, take this for now."

Martin's eyes went wide and took the proffered weapon. "Wow, thanks!" He held it gently in his hand, inspecting it under the lantern's fading light.

"You've used one before?"

"No, never."

Nate tapped the barrel of the pistol with a finger. "You point that at who I tell you to, okay?"

Martin barked a nervous laugh. "Yeah, okay." He squinted at it. "Is the safety on or off?"

Nate sighed. "Off. Just don't shoot yourself with it." You wouldn't be much use to me if you did, he thought.

"Okay," Martin said, and slid the pistol in the waistband of his pants. His soft, fat rolls nearly enveloped it. He may not be much of a gunman, but he was the only one Nate had at the moment.

"I think it would be best if we stuck it out here until morning," Nate said while Martin nodded in agreement. "Armed or not, it's too crazy out there to go traipsing around. And your lantern would draw too much attention to us, especially if someone wanted to take it."

"We got guns," Martin said, flush with his new responsibility. "They could try."

"Hopefully that stupid apartment building doesn't take this place down with it."

"I don't think so. It's pretty far over there."

They both sipped their beers. Nate considered practicing his new managerial style and broach the subject of Martin's sob story. He'd learn more about his underling and maybe get a better angle on how to keep him under control.

And if Nate didn't like what he heard, he could always shoot him.

"How did you get tangled up with the bear?" Nate asked.

"The bear? Oh, Unger. Yeah, that there was a real piece of work. And it actually wasn't me that got tangled."

"It wasn't?"

"No, it was my brother. He became an associate to that Morse guy and started to run errands for him."

"Poor bastard," Nate said. He couldn't imagine having that screw-up as a boss.

Martin nodded. "Had him running packets all over the city and into some really bad areas, too. Then after a while it progressed to stealing cars. My brother had a knack for that."

"Yeah? He jack a lot of good stuff?"

"Uh-huh, you name it, he could steal it. Alarms meant nothing to him. But it was when he stole a mercedes that something went wrong."

An alarm bell rang off in Nate's head. There was something familiar about this. "What happened? He get caught?"

"No," Martin said, his face grim. "He stole a mercedes that was the wrong color Unger wanted. Black instead of grey."

Now those alarm bells had turned into a full on klaxon. Nate swallowed his beer and waited for what he knew Martin would say next.

"Anyways, he brought this black mercedes into one of Unger's shops and when Unger found out the color, he went ballistic. Hated it and was crazy mad over the fact it wasn't grey. Unger actually made him take it back."

"Take the car back? From where he stole it?"

"Yeah, and it was there he was pinched by the cops. Kid had no choice but to take it back or he might get clipped from not following an order. So the kid gets thrown in jail, waiting to go to trial. While he was in there, Unger roped him into the drug market he was trying to start up. The kid tried to do it for a while, but it's rough in there and he couldn't keep up with the other dealers."

Martin went silent and Nate didn't pry. He knew this tale by heart.

After another sip, Martin said, "So he received a small shipment of crap from the outside, stuffed up a visitor's asshole. But before he could hide it, one of the other dealer's robbed him. Beat him up really good, too."

"And then your brother owed Unger for the missing drugs," Nate stated, matter-of-factly. It wasn't that he knew the details, it was just the natural progression of events in any criminal organization. You lose something the boss owns, you got to pay him back.

Martin nodded. "But before he could even start to try and pay Unger back, he got into a fight and was shanked. Bled out before anyone could help him. After that Unger said the debt was transferred to me. So he got me working for him for free, basically."

Nate gave him a few moments before asking, "What was your brother's name?"

"Ernie. Ernie Anway."

Well, this is awkward, Nate thought. He knew about Ernie Anway's death intimately, because he was the one who'd arranged it. Unger hated being owed by anyone, and if you took too long to pay, he had you eliminated as an example. Nate was under orders to have the guy killed, so he'd used his connections and got the job done.

Now he's sharing a beer with the dead man's brother. Nate took a sip to hide the smile that threatened to cross his face. This was just too funny.

To keep from laughing, he decided to get Martin out of the room. He pointed at the lantern which was dimming more by the minute. "You wouldn't happen to have more juice for this thing?"

Martin nodded, his face somber. "Sure. Brought a canister with me. Just a sec."

Nate watched the fat man walk outside and dig into the wheel-barrel. Now he was conflicted. It was obvious Martin didn't know of Nate's connection to Ernie's death, but that could change if he happened to talk to the wrong people. Then things would go from funny to fatal. Nate's first instinct was survival, which meant eliminating Martin, here and now.

Ah, too bad, Nate thought as he stood, taking a final sip from his beer. When Martin came back, he'd shoot him. After he filled the lantern, of course.

"Uh, boss?" Martin said from outside.

Nate looked over at him. Martin stared off into the darkness then gave a worried glance over his shoulder to Nate.

Nate grabbed the lantern and hustled to the front door, the shotgun in his free hand.

Once outside, Martin pointed. "Someone is coming."

Sure enough, several figures were walking across the parking lot toward the bar. Nate could see them because each one carried a flaming torch. As they got closer, he could also see they were armed, some with shotguns, others with automatic weapons.

Oh shit, Nate thought. It was too late to run, and too late to draw on them. He'd have to wait it out and see what the deal was.

Martin gave Nate a terrified look. "Do you recognize them?"

Nate looked at the approaching men. He could make out details, but he didn't know any of them. "No, do you?"

"Yeah," Martin said, nervous. "The big one there with the beard."

"Yeah, what about him?"

"That's Orson."

"So?"

Martin was trembling as he said, "Orson is Unger's little brother."

CHAPTER EIGHTEEN

Wyatt

"Save them?" Wyatt said. The words hung between he and Ethan like wet laundry. "That can't be it. How can I save anyone if I can't do the same for myself?"

Ethan shrugged. "Well, that is a good question. And one I hope will be answered soon."

"You don't have the answer? You're the asshole who said I had a job to do." As much as Wyatt wanted to doubt what Ethan was spewing, he felt deep down inside that his dead friend was right. That syrupy feeling returned.

"Hey, I'm just like anyone else, full of questions in search of answers. I can't hold both ends of the rope."

"What does that even mean?" Wyatt asked.

Ethan shook his head. "Look, Wyatt ol'buddy, I'd love to sit and chat with you some more, but you need to keep your head in the game. Sitting here in this truck will not bring you the answers you're looking for."

"Then where should I be?"

Ethan laughed. "Certainly not waiting for that security guard to figure out the police won't be coming to pick you up any time soon. They have their own problems, and besides, no one's told them what happened yet."

Wyatt looked at the guard, who was busy arguing with the man who pushed the woman. Ethan was right. No one knew what he'd done here. If he got away, maybe they would never know. How would they even identify him? Without power, any cameras that might have been able to record what happened didn't work anymore. And good luck getting someone to identify him in all this craziness. He could always shave his beard off, too.

"Don't do that," Ethan said.

Wyatt blinked at his friend. "Do what?"

"Shave your beard off. It gives you a noble visage."

"How did you know what I was thinking?" Wyatt said, alarmed.

Again, Ethan shrugged and Wyatt found the gesture annoying. "I don't have an answer for you on that, either," Ethan said. "But, hey, don't worry about me right now. You're going to miss your chance."

"Chance to what?"

"Escape," Ethan nodded to the guard.

Wyatt looked to see the large guard wrestling around the ground with the man he'd been arguing with. And then the woman who'd been pushed, jumped on the both of them. People shifted along the sidewalk trying to get out of the way.

"Time is wasting, buddy," Ethan said. "Can't let chance do all the work for ya."

Wyatt frowned at his dead friend's obtuse words then shifted around. With an effort, he turned his body and fell back onto the seat. He placed both of his frayed runners against the passenger side window.

"What are you doing?" Ethan said, curious.

"I'm breaking out!" Wyatt said, and kicked at the window. Nothing happened, so he did it again with both feet. The window held fast, so he kept hammering at it.

Ethan sighed. "Did you check to see if the door was locked?"

Wyatt paused in his assault. "Uh..." He shifted back up into a sitting position and glanced at the guard. The big man was still rolling around the sidewalk with both assailants.

Wyatt checked the door. It was unlocked. "Huh," he said as he shifted around so his hands could reach the door latch. "Why'd he do that?"

"You told him he'd let you go. Maybe that's why."

Wyatt eyed Ethan with suspicion. Ol'Eth was really full of it today, but he wouldn't argue with him. Whether intentional or not, the door was unlocked.

Carefully, he pulled at the latch and the door popped open. Wyatt held on tight so it wouldn't swing out and hit the car next to them.

The doctor came out of the clinic and started yelling at the guard. The guard paid him no mind and managed to get the woman pinned to the ground so he could put a set of plastic restraints on her. The other man sat propped up against the window, panting heavily, clutching his chest.

"Give it three seconds," Ethan said.

With the guard ignoring him, the doctor turned his attention to the truck and looked at Wyatt.

Wyatt froze and offered a dead eyed glare in return. He hoped the doctor didn't notice the door ajar in the growing darkness.

The doctor opened his mouth and pointed in Wyatt's direction.

Suddenly, the man clutching his chest cried out.

The doctor quickly turned his attention to the man and knelt next to him. He shouted for the nurse.

"Now would be good," Ethan said with a wide smile.

Wyatt eased the door open behind him and slowly slid out, keeping an eye on the confusion at the front of the truck. The truck's overhead light didn't turn on, for which he was grateful.

Placing one foot at a time onto the asphalt, Wyatt stood. The guard's back was turned, hunched over his new prisoner. The doctor and nurse performed CPR on the ailing man.

Concerned that trying to close the door would draw attention, Wyatt walked slowly backwards down the length of the truck. In seconds, he'd be out of sight and on his way.

Suddenly, Ethan leaned out of the open door and grinned at Wyatt. "Everything can't be easy!" He grabbed the door handle and slammed it shut.

The guard, who had stood up, whirled around. "Hey! Stop!"

Wyatt spun around and ran out past the truck and turned right. He raced down the length of the parking lot, hoping the cluster of people and cars would slow any pursuers.

His heart thudded in his chest and the restraints pinched deeper into his flesh with his frantic movements. A quick glance over his shoulder revealed the guard in hot pursuit. For such a big man, he was fast.

But Wyatt had the advantage. The sun had finally vanished behind the buildings. No street lights were turned on. In fact, there were no lights whatsoever. If it wasn't for the bright rash of stars across the sky, Wyatt wouldn't have been able to see a thing.

There was shouting behind him, but he didn't look. His concentration was fully on navigating the encroaching blackness. He swung around the strip mall, past more parked cars and along the side of the building. There were no lights here, either.

Wyatt slowed, unable to make out many details and not wanting to fall. His eyes needed to get used to the night.

A huffing and puffing made him look back.

The guard rounded the corner of the building. His large form was bulbous in the dark.

"Stop!" the big man shouted.

Wyatt had to give him credit, but increased his speed. He couldn't be caught. The guard would make sure another escape didn't happen. Besides, Wyatt had a mysterious job to do which probably did not entail being imprisoned.

He raced down the side of the building, maneuvering around vehicles which had stalled in the middle of the lane.

Wyatt felt invigorated. The last time he was chased had been years ago. The memory of a forest canopy winking with sunlight above played through his head.

Back then, his pursuers were just as dogged as the security guard. Only, death was their end game. Gunshots occasionally punctuated the air, breaking the monotony of his footfalls through the thick brush.

"Hunter One, do you copy, over?" someone said in his ear.

The voice sounded like Ethan's, but distorted. Taking a hand off his rifle, Wyatt tapped his ear mic. "I'm moving away from point, north by north-east," he said.

Static was the only answer. Wyatt raced down a rocky rise. In the distance, he heard a stream. Was that the one on the map? He couldn't be sure. The topography was as varied as it was beautiful.

He angled toward the sound of the running water. It might give him a proper location to find his pickup.

As he ducked under a low hanging branch, its bark shattered with a bullet's impact.

"Shit," he said, and tried to pick up the pace. They were close. Too close. Capture was not a good idea with these people. Death would be long in its arrival and would be most welcome when it did.

"Cancel pick up," the static voice said. "No go. New pick up to be determined."

Fear washed over Wyatt. No pick up? Then what was he running to?

Suddenly, a figure appeared deep within the trees to his right. It turned to aim a weapon at him.

With no time to think, Wyatt quickly raised his rifle and let out a short burst.

The figure fell back, his gun pinwheeling away.

Behind him, shouts, this time much closer than before. They got a lock on his position.

For a moment, he considered stopping and returning fire from cover. But the risk of being wounded and captured was too great.

"They peel the skin off you," Ethan said through the static in his ear. "You know that. You've seen it."

"Shut up," Wyatt said, huffing along. A pain stung his arms. He risked glancing down to find both his wrists were bleeding. What the hell? Did he get hit?

It was only the briefest of glances, but it took his eyes off the forest in front of him long enough for it to suddenly disappear.

Wyatt slid to a stop, the weight of his equipment and gear shifting on his body.

A wide river presented itself in all its raging glory. A steep embankment led down to its edge.

That ain't no stream, he thought. A branch close to his head suddenly exploded. Bark and chips of wood raked against the side of his face.

With nowhere else to go, Wyatt scrambled down the embankment, grabbing at anything to keep him from losing his balance and rolling.

Another shout, but he didn't look back. If he could get to the river he'd be safe. Or at least he would live a little longer.

As he stumbled to the river's edge, a burst of bullets created a spray of water from the river.

Wyatt jumped.

Cool water enveloped him and numbed his skin. Mountain streams were always the worst for that.

Wyatt kicked through the water, letting the current pull him along. His head bobbed to the surface, and he gasped for air.

A shout echoed through the trees, louder than the roaring water itself. Wyatt turned to look back as the forest sped past him.

The security guard stood on the concrete walkway along the river. His sweaty skin actually twinkled from the light of the stars above.

As the current carried Wyatt out of view, he heard Ethan in his ear. He tried to reach up to tap the ear mic, but found his arms couldn't move.

"You always were one for a dramatic exit," Ethan said.

CHAPTER NINETEEN

Nate

As the men approached, Nate counted seven of them.

Lucky number seven, he thought. Too many for him to handle at such close range, and especially with them so well armed. He saw no possible way out of this, considering he stood outside the bar where the bodies of Unger and his henchmen were sprawled in the back.

This was bad. Really bad.

Nate wanted to tell Martin to play it cool and let him do the talking. But there was no time and it would look suspicious to the other group. He only hoped his new underling had enough sense to keep his mouth shut and start firing when he did.

As they got within speaking distance, Nate casually placed the lantern on the ground and nodded to Orson. "Hello," Nate said, cool as can be.

The men spread out in a line, then stopped.

Orson, large, burly and bearded was the spitting image of his older brother. His expression was of suspicion. By way of greeting, he said, "Who the fuck are you?"

"Nate," Nate said. "This is Marty. We just got here and found the place empty. Know where Unger is?"

Orson eyed both of them up and down. "What the hell are you talking about, empty?"

"No one's around, so we were going to wait for Unger to get back," Nate said.

Each man held a torch out to his side, so the burning material didn't fall on them. In their other hands was a weapon. No one was pointing anything at Nate, yet. But that would change soon enough.

Orson glared at the two of them. Nate hoped that just by being present here at the bar showed he and Martin were Unger's men. If not, things would go south sooner than he liked.

"I don't know you, and I don't know you," Orson said, pointing at them in turn with a machine gun. "Where's Wilson and Earl? They should be on front door duty."

Martin started to sputter something out, but Nate cut him off. "I don't know. Like I said, we just arrived and found the place like this."

One of the men spoke up. "I know him," he said, nodding toward Martin.

"Oh, hey, Scott," Martin muttered with a smile like a rictus.

This took a little of the suspicion out of Orson's face, but he still scowled at them. Then he brushed past Nate and went into the bar. Three of the men followed him in.

Nate's heart pounded rapidly in his chest. He gave it twenty seconds before Orson found his dead brother, then five more before the shooting started.

"Bit of a messed up day, huh?" Martin said to Scott.

"Fuckin understatement," Scott said.

Everyone ignored the burning apartment building at the far end of the lot. Not their concern. Their concern was their boss.

Good, keep him distracted, lower his guard. Nate shifted a little so he could see Orson and his men move through the bar. They still clutched their torches which Nate thought odd. But he didn't care. Once they went into the office things would escalate quickly.

He had these three outside to contend with first. How things panned out with the remainder was up for debate. At least the group had split up.

Meanwhile, Martin kept talking. Whether it was a genuine attempt at distraction or just nervousness, Nate didn't care. It was working.

"Yeah, I had to walk all day to get here," Martin said, and gestured at the wheel-barrel full of prawns. "A real pain in the ass."

Scott snickered. "Yeah, Unger sure likes those things."

The other two men were eyeing Nate, but kept their guns down. They all may be one big happy criminal organization, but that didn't mean they had to completely lower their guard with each other.

"Tell me about it," Martin said, then launched into a spiel about his travels to get here.

As he spoke, Nate gave one final glance into the bar. Orson was in the office along with another man. The other two loitered outside the office door, torches held to their sides.

He saw Orson look in the direction of the hall and Nate could see the curious expression on his face. Orson moved out of sight.

Five seconds, Nate thought. He turned and suddenly made a show of looking into the distance behind the three men.

"Oh, shit, someone is coming," Nate said with the best impression of a worried underling he could muster.

All three men turned to look and, at that exact moment, Orson shouted from behind the back of the building. This caused Scott to rubberneck toward the front door.

Nate was already shooting.

His first target was the man closest to him. The shotgun ripped off the man's shoulder and sent him spinning backward.

Scott was already facing in the bar's direction, but reacted too slowly to raise his rifle. As Nate shot at him, Scott fired, but the bullet hit the concrete between Martin and Nate.

Nate had aimed for the other man's middle body mass, but ended up taking out his knees, instead. Scott screamed as he fell to the ground.

Amazingly, even as all this was happening in just a few seconds, Martin had the presence of mind to pull out his pistol from his waistband. He pointed it at the final man who let out a burst from his sub-machine gun.

Mercifully, the man's aim was bad. The burst hit the wall to one side of the front door.

But Martin's aim was impeccable. A single shot hit the last man almost between the eyes and he dropped to the ground like a marionette with its strings cut.

"Holy, shit!" Martin shouted as Nate grabbed him and pulled him out of view of the open doors. The men inside started firing.

Nate propelled them down the length of the building, away from the door. Martin let himself be pulled along, his face ashen with shock.

"I killed him," Martin said.

"We have to get to cover," Nate said, keeping an eye on the front door as they ran. When they reached the corner of building, he moved them around and out of view.

Martin squatted down and sat against the wall. Nate looked around the corner with one eye, watching for signs of pursuit.

"That was amazing," Martin said, shaking. The pistol was gripped tightly in his hand.

"Watch the trigger on that, will ya?" Nate said. "But you're right. That was pretty God-damned amazing what just happened. I thought we were as good as dead."

"Really?"

"Nah," Nate said with a grin. "I knew you could do it. Nice job distracting that one guy." Down by the front door, he could see their abandoned lantern lighting the area. Three torches lay by their dead owners corpses. One torch was close enough to catch Scott's shirt sleeve and set it on fire.

Beyond it all was the magnificent inferno that was the apartment building.

What a crazy scene, Nate thought, his heart hammering in his chest. And the first of many more to come.

"Yeah, I knew him from before," Martin said, his voice trembling with excitement. "Thought if I just-."

A head appeared out the bar's front door and Nate fired. The head ducked back inside. Nate didn't think he hit him, the shotgun was crap for accuracy at such a distance, but it kept the other man suppressed.

Martin quickly ducked into a crouch, pistol held up like one of those models you see on the covers of spy novels. "What is it? They coming?"

Nate shook his head, his eyes locked on the front door. "Not from this way." He glanced down the wall to the other corner of the building. The back lot was dimly lit by the distant apartment fire, but he could still see.

Martin suddenly pitched over, clutching his stomach.

"What? Did you get hit?" Nate asked.

Martin wretched, spewing a thick stream of vomit onto the ground.

Nate shook his head and kept watch. "The first time is always the hardest. You'll get used to it. Trust me."

Panting, Martin stood straight and wiped at his mouth. "Really? You got sick, too? It feels like I got a flock of angry birds fluttering around my stomach."

"Take a few deep breaths. They'll be coming at us soon," Nate said. The truth was, he didn't get sick when he made his first kill. In fact, he had been overjoyed. His father deserved what he got, so why should Nate have felt sick about it?

"They will?"

"I would," Nate said, casting another glance down to the other side corner. They were exposed from there. If Orson decided to flank them that's the direction he'd come.

"How many bullets do I have left?" Martin said, looking at his gun with mild confusion.

"Enough," Nate said. He reached over and pulled Martin by an arm. "Come here. Stand there and keep watch on the door. Shoot at anyone who sticks their head out, okay?"

Martin moved into position and peeked around the corner. He swallowed, blinking tears from his eyes.

"Stay solid," Nate said. He didn't need this guy to suddenly implode on him. He can do that later. "I'm going to check the other side."

"O-okay," Martin said, nervous. But he kept his eye on the front doors.

Nate stalked down the side of the building toward the other corner. When he got closer, he peeked around.

The moment he did, he saw a man skulking along the wall toward him, machine gun raised.

Nate fired his shotgun and ducked back. The other man fired and a burst of bullets peppered a line on the asphalt by Nate's feet.

"Whoa," he said, backing away and pressing up against the wall. Without looking, he stuck his shotgun around the corner and fired blindly.

A scream was his reward and Nate laughed. It had been a cowardly thing for him to do, but screw it. There were no rules when your life was on the line.

Another burst of fire, this going wide and hitting the wooden fence down at the other end of the lot. Nate looked the fence over. It was high with a stack of pallets nudged up against it. Beyond was a thin line of trees. Past that, he couldn't see in the darkness. A possible escape route.

He looked back at Martin. The man had not moved a muscle throughout the entire exchange, keeping his one eye locked on the front door. Nate felt a sudden burst of pride. This guy may not be a natural killer, but he was managing to keep his shit together fine enough.

A voice from around the corner called out. "You son of a bitch!"

It wasn't the man he'd just shot, too far.

"You killed my brother!" the voice shouted.

It was Orson. He sounded somewhere near the back door. Was there any cover down there? Nate couldn't remember. Maybe he could hide behind Unger's corpse. It was big enough.

"Why?" Orson wailed. "Why did you murder him?!"

Grinning, Nate shouted back, "He had shitty taste in beer!"

Suddenly, Martin fired the pistol, a single shot.

"We cool?" Nate called over to him.

Martin kept his pistol raised and his eyes widened. "I got him! I got another one!"

"Damn, soldier. Nice shooting," Nate said. If his math was right, that left two men, including cry-baby Orson. Nate's grin grew wider. This was shaping up better than he could have anticipated.

Not wanting Martin to have all the glory, Nate risked a quick peek around the corner.

Orson was ten feet away, running toward him, face filled with rage.

"Oh, shit!" Nate said, and fired. But Orson shot first.

Bullets hit the corner's edge, spraying pieces of brick into Nate's face.

With a shout of pain, Nate fell back, stumbled and landed on his back. He tried to open his eyes, but he couldn't see.

By the time he could blink away the crap in his face it was too late. Orson stood above him, machine gun pointed at Nate.

"You bastard!" Orson screamed. "You killed my brother! You're dead!" He raised his gun up a little and looked down the barrel at Nate.

Panic seized Nate, but he couldn't raise his shotgun. He was going to die.

Two shots rang out.

Orson grunted in pain, dropping his gun and clutched at his stomach. Blood gushed through his fingers. He looked up and past Nate.

Stunned, Nate looked, too.

Martin stood with the pistol in both hands, legs spread apart like he was in a shooting range.

"Fuck you and your brother," Martin said, and fired again.

This bullet hit Orson in the forehead and the big man fell backwards on the ground, dead.

Martin ran over to Nate. "You okay, boss?"

Nate blinked at the pain that burned across his face. "Yeah, I'll live. Thanks."

As Martin tried to help him up, Nate waved him away. "There's still one guy left. Watch that door!"

Martin nodded and ran back to the corner. The moment he peered around it, he raised his pistol and fired again, shouting in surprise.

A scream of pain was followed by a burst of gunfire. Martin ducked back behind the building as bullets tore through the brickwork.

Nate pushed himself up to his feet, shotgun still in hand. He looked at Martin with concern. "You okay?"

Martin blinked in amazement and looked his body over. "Yeah! Not a scratch."

The screaming continued then died down.

"I'm gonna finish this," Martin said and Nate didn't argue.

With another quick look, Martin could see that the other man was dying on the ground, and no longer a threat. He calmly raised his pistol, aimed, and fired.

"That's that," Martin said as Nate hobbled over.

"That was all of them," Nate said, and tried to grin, but the pain of his face made him wince.

Martin cringed when he looked at him. "Damn, boss. Looks like your face is messed up."

"At least it's not my pride," Nate said. He looked down the front of the building.

Two more bodies had been added to the carnage. One at the front door, the other about half way down the building. Nate shook his head.

Imagine that. Martin pulled his weight and then some. Now he was glad he hadn't killed him earlier. Without him, this show would have ended a lot differently.

Smoke began to froth out the front doors of the bar.

"It's burning," Martin said.

Nate said, "That's *Spectacular*." He winced as he tried to laugh at his own stupid joke. "Come on, let's grab as much of their stuff as we can carry."

"And then what?" Martin asked, eagerness on his face.

"Then we start to build an empire."

CHAPTER TWENTY

Wyatt

There were no more trees, just towering buildings, dark and cold. Had they even been there?

Did he just run through a forest, bullets flying all around? He couldn't remember.

The sound of rushing water roared in his ears.

He was on the side of a river bank which snaked its way through the city. The rumbling waters vanished into the black maw of a tunnel, a short distance from where he was. Hard concrete pressed against his body, not the soft, wet dirt of a forest. His clothes were soaked through, but he didn't mind.

I escaped, he thought.

Looking to his right, he could see the dark outline of the river curving around a bend, the direction he must have come from. This was not a natural river, but one guided by the hand of man.

He peered up and found himself breathless at the sight of so many stars. The sky was stunningly clear.

Another memory tried to bubble up from the depths of his mind, but he forced it down. Enough of that.

He tried to stand up, only to realize his hands were still bound behind his back. The cold water had frozen him so thoroughly, he couldn't feel them anymore.

With a sluggish effort, he shook his head and blinked his eyes. Water soaked his beard. He had to get up, get moving. Sitting here will only complicate things, give his enemies time to catch up.

But who were they?

"Smarten up!" Wyatt said, his voice fighting to be heard over the river's frothy roar. His eyes drooped. What was wrong with him?

He needed to stand up. Now.

Slipping one foot beneath his butt, he tried to stand. Half way to his goal, he lost all balance and fell over on his side.

He coughed and wretched, water spraying from his mouth. He must have swallowed half the river.

For a few moments, he lay there, watching the river pass by. The sounds of its passage echoing loudly from the tunnel.

"Where's the pick up?" he asked. He almost expected to hear a static filled answer in his ear, but none came.

An image of the security guard stalking up behind him made Wyatt suddenly roll over. This time, he felt his arms and the plastic restrainers which cut into them. No guard was there. He was further up the river.

Wyatt looked up the concrete embankment which extended to a chain-link fence. Behind the fence was a dumpster, its rectangular form nearly blending into the night.

"Huh," Wyatt said. "Maybe I'll find some cans." But he didn't try to get up, again. In fact, he didn't want to get up any more. He decided he'd done enough movement for one day. Why do more? What was it good for?

Today, he watched his friend die after trying for hours to find him help. What a waste.

He'd killed two people. Feral Kids, sure. But still people.

No, he thought. Not people, a start. Didn't he say that to the security guard?

Wyatt realized that something was wrong with him. Really wrong. Not a passing phase or a late mid-life crisis or any of that nonsense. Something was rotten in Denmark.

Another memory tried to peek around the corner of his mind, but he swatted it away. None of that now.

He'd just rest here a while and watch the waters stream by.

Waters stream by. Ha-ha. Ethan would like that one.

As his eyes began to close, a light appeared. From his position on the ground, he titled his head back to look in the direction of the tunnel.

A light was in there, deep inside. Small, but bright against the eternal blackness.

As Wyatt watched, the light moved, bobbing and weaving in a little dance.

His mind was empty of thought, only the light mattered. Its approach was calming, soothing.

Soon the light breached the mouth of the tunnel and Wyatt saw that it was a man carrying a lantern.

The man paused and looked around, holding the lantern up in front of him.

Wyatt thought he recognized him.

"Ethan?" he said, unsure, and suddenly coughed up more water. When his spasm had passed, he discovered the man standing above him, smiling down.

"What's up, ol'buddy?" Ethan said with a wide grin. "Took a spill into the drink, did you?"

Wyatt glared angrily up at him. "You know I did. It was your idea!"

"Was it? I dunno about that," Ethan said. He bent over and helped Wyatt into a sitting position.

The movement made Wyatt dizzy. "Why did you slam that door?"

"What door?" Ethan asked. He settled down next to Wyatt and placed the lantern between them. It was an old kerosene lamp.

"You know what I mean. I was almost scott-free, but you had to go and ruin it."

Ethan shook his head, an expression of pity on his face. "Wyatt, I didn't slam any door."

"Yeah, you did," Wyatt said, and spit out some more river water. "I was following your little escape plan and then you went and made things..."

"What?"

"Complicated!"

Ethan chuckled. "Well, what happened in the past, stays in the past. Right? What matters is you're here now. Safe." He gave Wyatt a friendly nudge. "Don't be angry. You know it doesn't suit you."

"Suits me just fine," Wyatt said. He felt that syrupy feeling creeping up on him again. Threatening to make him talk funny. He tried to shake it away. "I'm messed up, Ethan." The admission made him feel a little better. Less weight on his mind.

Ethan nodded. "I am well aware. But you're going to be even more messed up if we don't find a way to get those restraints off you. Can't do your new job all trussed up like a Sunday ham."

"Saving people?" Wyatt said.

His dead friend only shrugged. "Something like that. Like I said. I only have questions or answers, not both." He pushed himself up to his feet and grabbed the lantern. "You coming?"

"Coming where?" Wyatt said, suspicious.

Ethan pointed to the tunnel. "In there, stupid."

Wyatt arched a brow. "I don't like the dark."

"That's what makes you perfect for your new job."

"Why?"

"Because you will do all you can to find the light," Ethan said, and motioned for Wyatt to stand. "Come on, get up. The future has already started and you're going to miss out."

That syrupy feeling edged over Wyatt's shoulders, up his neck and across his scalp. "Yeah, maybe." He tried to stand again, using his legs, but couldn't do it.

"Mind helping me out a little?" Wyatt said.

Ethan's smile was wide and for the briefest of moments, he looked just like Santa Claus. He stuck a hand under Wyatt's arm. "No, Wyatt. I don't mind one bit."

Finally standing, Wyatt rocked back and forth on the balls of his feet, trying to get the circulation back in his legs. It was damned cold out.

"Okay, now where?" Wyatt said, eyeing the tunnel.

"We go to the end of that," Ethan said, nodding toward the opening. He starting guiding Wyatt forward.

"And what's down in there?"

"Answers, maybe."

"In a tunnel?"

Ethan laughed. "Hey, don't knock it until you've reached the end."

As they crossed over the entrance, Wyatt peered ahead with suspicion. "I'm not sure about this, Ethan."

Ethan shrugged, the light from the lantern seemed to be absorbed into his white beard. "To be honest, I'm not sure about this, either."

They walked further along, the river roiling in the dark beyond the edge of the lantern's light.

Wyatt eyed Ethan then asked, "What sort of answers will I find down there?"

Ethan smiled and his teeth practically twinkled like the stars outside. "I think the first answer will be the most important and I believe we'll find it soon it enough."

"Wait," Wyatt said with unabashed confusion. "What the hell is the question?"

"How do we begin to save the world?"

CHAPTER TWENTY ONE

Nate

"Go ahead and dump those prawns out," Nate said.

Martin grinned. "With pleasure." He hefted the wheel-barrel and the plastic bags slid onto the ground in a pile.

"See," Nate said with a smile. "Hauling that crap all the way here paid off, but not how you expected."

"Yup," Martin said. "I gotta be honest, this day hasn't shaped up the way I thought it would."

Both of them laughed.

The fire inside the bar was in full force, with flames consuming everything inside. Thick smoke billowed out from the doors.

They backed up several paces then took a few minutes to watch the bar burn.

"So much for sticking it out here," Martin said. He was still jacked up on adrenaline from the fight. Nate knew it could be hours before he came down from that wonderful high.

"That is a problem," Nate said. "I know our friends here will have more coming at some point. Whether tonight or in the morning is anyone's guess."

"Orson had a big crew," Martin said and coughed a little from the smoke. "At least thirty guys or so."

Nate had never encountered Orson before tonight, much to Orson's demise. He'd heard of the big bastard many times. Just as mean and cruel as his brother. But he was a part of the organization, too. At some point, they will come around to check in. The best thing to do is leave. Now.

"I don't know about you, but I've had enough gun-play for one night."

Martin laughed. "I dunno. I think I can take out a few more for you if you wanted."

Nate smiled. Yeah, this one is a keeper, that's for sure. "We best put some distance between us and this little mess we created. Grab all these guns and whatever else might be useful. I'll go back and get Orson's and the other weapons."

After a few minutes they collected seven guns and four pistols along with lots of extra ammo. Nate made a point of taking the money out of all their wallets, too. You never know.

Martin looked down at all the weaponry in the wheel-barrel. "Think this will help with our empire?"

Our empire? Nate thought. He let it slide. "Not even close. Not without trusted hands that can hold them." He nodded to a small satchel at Martin's feet. "What's that?"

"This here was under that first guy you blew away," Martin said, opening it. It was full of torches.

"Nice," Nate said. "These guys got their shit together fast. Made these torches when they realized there's no other means of light."

"And now they're ours," Martin said, placing the satchel into the wheel-barrel. Then he picked the wheel-barrel up by its handles. "Where to, boss?"

Nate picked up the lantern which Martin had refilled from a small canister. He had decided to carry the AK-47 Orson had tried to kill him with and slung the shotgun under his jacket. "We need to find a place to hang out for a while, until morning. Maybe longer. Do you know this area at all?"

"Nope, I just come here to make deliveries. Or I used to. No more of that crap."

Nate let him revel in his perceived freedom. "Let's walk and see what we can see. Maybe an opportunity will present itself."

They crossed the parking lot and away from the burning bar.

"I saw a bicycle back there. That yours?" Martin asked as he huffed along.

"It was a gift from a stranger."

"You could ride it," Martin said. "I don't mind."

Nate nearly laughed out loud at that. Instead, he said, "Nah, no more bikes for me." Soon, if I wanted to go somewhere, I'll have someone carry me, he thought with a smile.

They left Spectacular's parking lot and moved into the street. On a whim, Nate turned them northward, and they kept walking. This led past the front of the burning apartment building. Some people were here, clustered on the opposite side of the road, staring mournfully at their burning homes. When they saw Nate and Martin coming, most backed away or simply turned and fled.

"Our fireworks got them spooked," Martin said.

As they walked by, Nate felt that invigorating surge return. Here he was walking down the street armed to the teeth and not giving a damn what anyone thought. What could they do about him?

Martin must have felt something too because he stuck out his chest and sneered at anyone they passed.

"This is definitely a new era we're entering into, boss," Martin said after several streets. There were stranded cars everywhere, but none with drivers. Everyone must have decided to trek home before it got too dark.

"Yup," Nate said. "I'm liking how it's starting out so far."

They laughed.

"Hey, what's that?" Martin said, nodding his head further down the street.

A strange light was bobbing along on the sidewalk in their direction.

"I have no idea," Nate said. They stopped and waited to see what the deal was.

As the strange light got closer, they could see it was two young women walking toward them. In their hands, they each clutched a large batch of glow-sticks which gave off just enough illumination to see where they were going.

The two girls noticed the weaponry in the wheel-barrel and the AK Nate carried. They stopped, stunned.

"Hello, ladies," Nate said as he approached them. Martin put down his burden and followed.

"Hello," one of the women said, a blonde.

"Whatcha got there?" Nate asked about the sticks.

"These are party sticks. We use them at clubs, but realized they'd do well at night since everything doesn't work anymore."

Nate chuckled. "Well, isn't that clever," he said, inspecting the sticks closely. There were several colors and gave off a dreamy neon glow. "Better than nothing, huh?"

The other girl, a brunette, giggled nervously. She was also carrying a paper bag full of groceries.

"Whatcha got there?"

The brunette giggled again, a sound Nate didn't find very attractive, then she said, "We got these from the store up the street."

"How the hell did you pay for them?"

"Cash."

Nate laughed. "Of course, the good old-fashioned way."

Encouraged by Nate's demeanor, the brunette said, "Yeah, the cashier had to add it up on a piece of paper and everything. Wasn't too hard."

"My friend and I are a little hungry. Got anything in there worth sharing?" Nate added just a hint of menace to his words.

The women stood paralyzed for a few moments, then the blonde said, "Sure. We got chips and coke."

"I'm starving," Martin said, but his eyes were not on the food.

The women looked at him fearfully.

"Care to share?" Nate said.

"Sure," the blonde said. Hastily, the women empty the bag and handed over the food.

Martin cracked open a can and guzzled the contents down in several long swallows. Then he tossed the can onto the street where it clattered and rolled away.

"My friend here has worked up quite the thirst," Nate said.

Martin burped loudly then ripped open a chip bag. He began devouring them in large handfuls.

Nate did the same, but with a more civil approach, sipping from his can and eating chips one at a time.

The women watched them, wide eyed and apprehensive. Eventually, the blonde worked up the courage to speak. "Well, we got to be going now. Our friends are waiting. Glad we could help you out."

As they started to move away, Nate casually lifted up his AK. The girls stopped. "No need to go just yet," he said around a mouthful chips. "Where are you two going, anyway?"

"Home," the blonde said.

"How far?"

The answer took several moments in coming. "About four blocks from here."

"You live with your friends?"

"Yeah, we share a house together."

"How many?"

Another long pause. "Five of us. Why?"

"Just wanted to know who I'll be meeting, is all." He motioned with is AK for them to start walking. "Why don't you take us to your friends. We'll make sure we don't eat all their chips."

Now petrified, the women could do nothing other than what they were told. They continued on down the sidewalk, this time with Nate behind them, munching chips. Martin followed along on the street, pushing the wheel-barrel.

They passed houses where people huddle outside around makeshift fires or inside with candles. Anyone who saw them zeroed in on Nate and Martin and then vanished from view.

If the women were hoping someone might intervene on their behalf, they were wrong.

Eventually they arrived at a cute two-story house. In the small front yard, three people were sitting around a large mound of glow-sticks talking and laughing.

Nate looked them over. Two red-headed babes and a gawky looking guy.

As they got closer, the people looked in their direction. Their expressions morphed into concern once they noticed Nate's AK.

Nate's group walked up onto the yard. "Howdy," he said, cheerfully.

The others stood up, the two red-heads clutching at each other. The blonde and brunette ran over to them.

"These guys took our food!" the brunette said. "I think they want to rob us."

"No, there will be no robbing," Nate said with a smile. "You're too pretty for that."

The gawky guy walked up to Nate despite his weapon. "You guys need to leave. You're not welcome here."

Nate couldn't tell if this guy was brave or stupid. He settled on stupid. "Now that's not very friendly of you, is it? My friend and I need a place to hang out for a while. We thought we'd crash at your place. Your house is big enough."

The guy put up a blustering front, probably to impress the girls. "I said you're not welcome here. Leave."

"No," Nate said.

Shaking with agitation the guy said, "Who the hell do you think you are, fucker?"

"Who do I think I am?" Nate asked.

He shot the guy with a single burst from the AK, nearly cutting him in half. The women screamed in terror.

Nate looked them all over and smiled.

"Why... I'm your new king."

CHAPTER TWENTY TWO

Wyatt

"Are we there, yet?" Wyatt said.

They had been walking for what seemed like hours, but Wyatt couldn't be sure. Time had lost all meaning once the entrance to the tunnel vanished from view.

"Almost," Ethan said. He held the lantern high, its bright light creating glittery stars across the river next to them.

"You haven't said anything in ages," Wyatt said, casting his dead friend a suspicious look. "What are you up to?"

"Nothing," Ethan said. "If anything, you are the one that is up to something. I'm just helping you along."

"Okay, whatever," Wyatt said. The syrupy feeling that had enveloped him was gone. Now his mind was free to dance around all sorts of crazy thoughts. "You were always evasive, you know that?"

"What do you mean?"

"You know what I'm saying. You never shared with me your past or anything you were thinking beyond the next dumpster. Even after all these years."

Ethan scoffed. "I need secrets, too, you know. You can't corner the market on that. Other people have things they don't want to talk about, either."

"You're avoiding the question."

"No, I'm not. I'm choosing not to answer it, that's all."

They walked on in silence for a while. The tunnel did not vary in direction one degree, just a straight line. Nor did it dip downward, for which Wyatt was actually grateful for. He was hoping to get out of this place soon enough.

"My arms hurt," Wyatt said for the twentieth time.

"And you know I can't do anything to help with that," Ethan said. "We'll get those restraints off when we find some help."

"Is that what we're doing? Finding help? I thought we were looking for answers to questions, or some such nonsense."

Ethan didn't respond, only kept moving forward. Wyatt had little choice but to follow along.

After a while, Ethan said, "I was an accountant."

Wyatt was poleaxed by this revelation. "No way! A numbers guy?"

Ethan nodded.

Wyatt shook his head. "That's amazing. You never struck me as the office type."

Ethan scoffed. "An office is its own kind of dumpster, believe-you-me. But if I had a choice between running reports all night in time for the month end cash flow or rolling around in garbage, I'd take the garbage option every time."

Wyatt walked along in stunned silence. Then he said, "How much did you make?"

"Salary? More than cans and bottles."

"No, seriously."

Ethan was quiet a moment, then said, "Six figures a year. Not including bonuses."

Wyatt laughed, looking at his friend in unabashed amazement. "I don't believe it. Six God-damned figures a year. And now you're... you're... uh."

"Dead?" Ethan finished for him.

"Yeah, dead. Sorry about that."

"You have absolutely nothing to apologize for. What happened, happened. There's no going back."

Wyatt shook his head. "Yeah, but if I had handled those Feral Kids differently, maybe things would have turned out another way."

Ethan shook his head. "No, it wouldn't have."

"What do you mean?"

Ethan stopped, catching Wyatt off guard for a second and nearly causing him to fall into the river.

"Whoa, hey!" Wyatt said. The river raged by, the lantern light creating silver serpents across its surface.

"Things were not meant to turn out differently," Ethan said, his eyes never leaving Wyatt's. "They happened the way they were intended to."

"I don't get it," Wyatt said. He could feel the drying blood from his wrists on the small of his back, thick and sticky.

Ethan sighed, closing his eyes.

Wyatt waited, not sure what his friend was up to.

Ethan opened his eyes and looked at Wyatt. "If I hadn't had died then I wouldn't have been in any position to guide you. We would still be out there jumping into dumpsters and counting pennies."

"There's nothing wrong with that. Dumpster diving, I mean."

"No, but you were meant for more than that and you know it."

Wyatt mulled that over. "About that. What's with me dipping in and out of... I don't know how you would describe it..."

"Crazy?"

"Yeah, crazy. Why is that happening? It never happened before."

"That you remember."

This just confused Wyatt more. "Now I'm all turned around. You mean I've slipped into crazy-town before? Before today?"

Ethan watched his friend, the lantern making his eyes appear like black pits. "Yes, Wyatt. You have. Many times. Now, can we continue on? We're almost there."

He continued walking, but it was the last sentence that snagged Wyatt's attention. "We're almost out of here? Really?"

"Yes."

"How do you know? How do you know any of this?"

"You want to know the secret as to how I know we're almost out of here?"

"Yeah, tell me."

Ethan pointed. "Because there's the exit up ahead."

Wyatt looked. Sure enough, the tunnel ended a short distance away. Somewhere beyond it, an orange glow highlighted the exit's shape.

"Oh, thank God!" Wyatt said, and picked up the pace. Ethan trailed along.

Wyatt ran past the lantern's light radius.

"Be careful, Wyatt. Don't fall into the river, again. You definitely wouldn't survive it a second time."

Wyatt ignored him and rushed ahead, his panting breath loud in his ears, canceling out the roaring of the river.

Soon, he stood at the tunnel terminus. The river dropped here and rushed down into the darkness of the world outside. To one side, there was a wide concrete plateau which revealed a dry spillway. Beyond that, he could see tall buildings, dark against the starry sky.

A large campfire was in the middle of the spillway. A figure sat next to it.

"We're out!" Wyatt said, and turned to Ethan.

Only Ethan wasn't there. Nor was his lantern light. Just pitch darkness and the sound of the river within.

"Ethan?" he said, looking around. "Where the hell did you go, now?"

Ethan didn't reappear.

Frustrated, Wyatt navigated his way down to the spillway toward the campfire. As he got closer, the figure became more familiar.

At the edge of the fire's light, Wyatt stopped in amazement. "Baldy?"

The figure turned and looked at him in surprise.

"W-Wyatt?" Baldy exclaimed. He got up and ran over to Wyatt. "Are you o-okay? You look like complete sh-sh-sh-."

"Shit, yes, Baldy, I do, and I feel it."

Baldy guided Wyatt over to the fire, a huge grin on his face. "B-boy it's real g-good to see you. I've b-been worried."

Wyatt plopped down next to the fire, getting as close to its warmth as he dared. "Worried? Why? Last time I saw you we were making our rounds." That seemed like a lifetime ago, instead of a single day.

Baldy looked at Wyatt like he was nuts. He raised his arms and said, "The world has g-gone crazy, Wyatt. E-everyone's freaking out ab-about the power. I thought something might have h-happened to you and Ethan."

Wyatt frowned. "Oh, that. Nothing to worry about." He didn't want to talk about Ethan right that very moment. "Hey, you got a knife or some scissors?"

Baldy blinked in confusion then pulled out a huge butcher knife from a side pocket. "L-like this?"

Ethan's worries about Baldy being a mass murderer played through Wyatt's mind. "Uh, yeah. Mind cutting these damned restraints off my arms for me?"

Baldy lit up like a child on christmas morning. "S-sure, lemme get 'em for you."

As Baldy sawed at the restraints, Wyatt tried not to let himself get too worried. He doubted Baldy was a mass murderer. Or, at least for the next few moments he wasn't.

There was an audible snip from behind Wyatt and suddenly his hands were free. "Oh, thank God!" Wyatt said as he rubbed at his arms. They were cold and numb.

Baldy moved to the fire, smiling like a fool. "Want some c-coffee. Just made it."

"Hell, yeah!" Wyatt said as he examined the wounds on his wrists. The restraints had really cut into him.

Baldy handed him a tin cup full of piping hot coffee. Wyatt sipped at it eagerly.

"Baldy, this is the best coffee I've ever had. Thank you."

"R-really?"

"Yup," Wyatt said, drinking. Soon his gaze sank into the fire.

After a time, Baldy started to get worried. "Are you okay, W-Wyatt? Your f-face looks kinda f-funny."

That syrupy feeling had arrived again and washed over Wyatt like a slow tsunami. "Yeah, I'm fine. Just fine."

After a few moments, Baldy asked. "Whatcha th-thinking about?"

"Oh, my new job. I figured it out now. What it is."

"Yeah? Wh-what's your job?"

When Wyatt looked to Baldy, Baldy couldn't be certain the face he saw was Wyatt's at all.

"My job?" Wyatt said, his voice hollow and distant.

"My new job is to save the world."

To Be Continued In

The Second Day

www.ingramcontent.com/pod-product-compliance
Lightning Source LLC
Chambersburg PA
CBHW071750150726
47998CB00005B/1873